EGGS IN ONE
BASKET

ALSO BY KATHY MACKEL

CAN OF WORMS

KATHY MACKEL

■ HarperCollins*Publishers*

Library of Congress Cataloging-in-Publication Data
Mackel, Kathy.
    Eggs in one basket / Kathy Mackel.
        p.   cm.
    Summary: With the help of two middle school classmates and a
bear-like talking "dog" from the planet Sirius, seventh-grader Scott
Schreiber discovers that he can be a hero in other ways than on the
football field.
    ISBN 0-380-97847-4 — ISBN 0-06-029213-X (lib. bdg.)
    [1. Extraterrestrial beings—Fiction.   2. Schools—Fiction.
3. Heroes—Fiction.   4. Science fiction.]   I. Title.
PZ7.M1955 Eg   2000   00-27118
[Fic]—dc21   CIP
                                                              AC

2   3   4   5   6   7   8   9   10
❖

TO CASEY AND ERIN

ACKNOWLEDGMENTS

TO SUE CLARK FOR ALL HER
SUPPORT AND ADVICE.

EGGS iN ONE
BASKET

1

THE CROWD ROARED AND MY HEART roared back. This is what I was born for, what I lived for. Football.

It was a cold Friday night, the last regular game of the season. We were tied for first place with Bristol Middle School. The winner would advance to the Super Bowl on the day after Thanksgiving. The loser would be the turkey.

The Bristol players scurried onto the field, looking like dung beetles in their ugly brown uniforms. The thugs from Bristol munched garlic, raw potatoes, and cooked spinach before each game. Their coach's lame health concoction made them reek like the bottom of the school cafeteria's Dumpster. They stunk up the field with their reeking breath.

All the more reason to mow them down.

The announcer called our names. My teammates took the field, one by one, until I was the only player left.

"And . . . now, introducing . . . Ashby's all-time passing leader. Ashby's all-time rushing leader . . ." The roar intensified, a tidal wave of excitement. ". . . Conference All-Star . . ." The cheers were like a solid wall, pushing me through the victory gauntlet: the grinning coaches, the flushed cheerleaders, my pumped teammates. "Number thirteen . . ." I high-fived down the row, past LeSieur, Crisostamo, Hardy. Even Mike Pillsbury growled as he pounded me five.

"Quarterback . . . SCOTT SCHREIBER!"

The field exploded with drums, stomping, and trumpets. Nothing would stop the Mighty Schreiber, not tonight. Not any night.

I gathered the team at the bench. "What're we gonna do?" I bellowed.

"Win!" my team yelled back. Across midfield, the Bristol huddle looked like a manure pile, ready to be plowed under.

"I can't hear you!"

"WIN!" they screamed louder.

I turned to the home bleachers. "What're we gonna do tonight?"

"WIN!" the Ashby fans shouted back. The cheer-leaders took up the chant. "WIN WIN WIN!"

This was what I was born for: the roar of the crowd, the heat of the game, the smell of victory. I waved my hands over my head, stirring up the chant. WIN WIN WIN! I revved the crowd higher and louder until—

Eeeeeeeeeeeyoooooooooooowwwwwwwwwwl!!!!!!!!!

—my head was split by a bolt of screeching sound. Driving from ear to ear, a noise like strangled sirens ripped through my brain.

"What's wrong, Scott?" Pillsbury whispered as I slumped to the bench.

"Don't you hear that?" I moaned.

"Hear what? What's the matter? You're white like a ghost," he said.

"And you're a pain like a butt. I mean, in the butt." I strapped on my helmet. The lightning screech rattled my head again. "What the heck is that noise?"

"It's the band. Allegedly playing." Pillsbury laughed, probably happy because the one kind of geek he was *not* was a band geek.

"They stink! Tell them to shut up!"

"Since when are you a music critic? Besides, it makes them feel important. Makes us want to kill, kill, kill."

"I'll kill all right. I'm gonna shove those horns down their throats and those clarinets up their—"

Again, the screech rattled my teeth. My insides

3

twisted and I clamped my mouth shut. No way I was going to puke in public just because some band bozo couldn't blow a decent note.

As our coaches went out to confer with the referees, I climbed into the bandstand. Ducking trombones and weaving around the tubas, I gunned for the screech-meister who was slaughtering my ears.

There she was, in the back row. Shaggy brown bangs. Pudgy cheeks that dimpled every time she sucked in air. Dark, round eyes with lashes that flapped constantly, like a neurotic butterfly. She huffed and puffed with total but useless concentration.

A Weird Band Girl.

I clenched my hands; otherwise I would rip that thing out of the Weird Band Girl's mouth and bash it over her head. "Hey you. Excuse me? Hey! YOU!"

She peered over her music holder. A string of spit dripped from her mouth as she pulled the instrument away. "Yeth?" she lisped as she slurped the saliva back. "What do you want?"

"You want us to win tonight. Right?" I faked a cheery smile.

She tooted agreement. My head almost blasted off. "STOP!" I screamed. Three flute girls turned to look. One smiled, the other two blushed. I have that effect on girls.

Except this Weird Band Girl—she showed me no

respect. "Do you have a problem with my playing?" she asked.

"No, of course not. It's just that . . ." *Think Schreiber. Another toot and you're done for.* "I always ask a band member to sit it out. For really awesome luck. Tonight's your special night."

"My special night? Oh, be still my heart. Some football pseudo-hero charges into the band with a moronic request and I'm supposed to drop everything?"

"Look, give me a break. I need you to do this for me."

"Why should I do anything for you?"

"Because I'm the Mighty Schreiber."

She stared at me through those flapping eyelashes like I was a bug on the end of her nose. "And the Mighty Schreiber is . . . what?" she said. "Not a disease, I hope."

The band geeks around me giggled.

"Ashby's finest!" I said, too loud.

The music started up again and she joined them. I squeezed my eyes against the tears of pain. Some hero—crying in the middle of the marching band. I put my hand over the end of her instrument, wincing at the hot air coming out, hoping she wouldn't dribble spit on me. "Look, if you won't do it for me, could you do it for the good of Ashby Middle School?"

The Weird Band Girl stopped playing. "So whatever the Mighty Schreiber wants, the Mighty Schreiber gets?"

I flashed my best winning QB smile. "If it's good for the team."

She put down her instrument of torture. "Fine. Whatever. I'm bored with this infantile music anyway."

I thumbs-upped her, then ran to the Ashby bench, ready to crush the bugs from Bristol.

We were getting crushed.

The score was Bristol 14, Ashby 10, less than a minute to go. Only ten men grouped in my offensive huddle. "Where's Tenore?" I snarled.

Pillsbury pushed his way into the circle. With his sports goggles and string bean legs, he looked like something from outer space. "He's getting his ankle X-rayed."

"Clark?"

"His elbow's icing."

"Fleming?"

Pillsbury grimaced. "They're still looking for his front teeth near the forty-yard line. They think they can implant them back in . . ."

The garlic-spewing thugs from Bristol were running us down like roadkill. Six of my teammates had been carried off the field with sprained and bruised body parts. I had been sacked more times in this game than I had all season. If Bristol didn't kill my front line, I was going to.

"So who is Coach sending in for center?"

"Um . . ."

"No. Tell me no."

"I'm the last one left standing. Coach says to try the new decoy play and . . ." Pillsbury's voice trailed off.

"And what!"

"And pray," Pillsbury whispered. "Pray."

I stifled a moan. "Okay, men. Ain't nothing left in life but that goal line. Let's go get it." I clapped my hands and we scattered. The blockers hulked down on the front line. Pillsbury perched in the middle like a scrawny squirrel in the headlights of a speeding truck.

As Coach Tremblay had advised, I prayed: *Don't let the little nerd snap it over my head, don't let him fumble, don't let him soak the ball in sweat so it slips out of my hands, don't let him get trampled, don't let HIM let ME get trampled.*

"Hut one, nine, four, break!" I barked.

The ball was in my hands and the Bristol stink bombs were coming down my throat. Keras stepped to my left and I faked a handoff. As the defensive line shifted, I lateralled right to DuCharme. Pillsbury and Conner were supposed to open a hole in the middle . . . yeah, there it was. Conner grunted and shoved two goons while Pillsbury backpedaled, some gorilla rolling over him to get to me. DuCharme faked left, then lateralled back to me. I wrapped my forearm around the ball and charged at that tiny hole before Conner and Pillsbury got trampled.

Open field! Thirty yards away, glowing under the lights, the end zone and our ticket to the Super Bowl! I pumped hard, keeping the ball tight against my ribs. My feet flew over the turf, the grass flew under my feet, the crowd flew by as I . . .

. . . *flew. The world was green and peaceful under my wings and the sun was bright and full of promise. But my heart was heavy. Our enemies, folk we had never met and never wronged, pursued me across the skies. I alone held the promise for my people's future and they were gaining on me, intent on . . .*

. . . on ripping the ball from my hands! What the heck! While I'd been daydreaming, the slugs from Bristol were jamming down my throat! A brown-shirted safety pounded on my right while a foul-smelling tight end roared from my left. The goal line was steps away and I could see the future: my bones crushing, my head exploding, and the ball popping out of my arms.

I went vertical—over the colliding Bristol defenders and into the end zone. Touchdown! I saw glory, I saw victory, I saw the Super Bowl!

And then I saw stars.

2

THE GREATEST MOMENT OF MY LIFE

and I lay flat on my back, straddling a bedpan. My neck was taped in a brace and a bag of ice dripped down my head. Outside the curtain, some high school volunteer waited for me to pee in the pot. I should have been carried off the field on the shoulders of my team. Instead, my urine would be paraded down the hall of Ashby Medical Center.

All because I saw stars.

"Stars!" I had said to Coach Tremblay an hour earlier, as he helped me up in the end zone.

"Jeepers, you seein' stars?" the coach growled. "Don't get up yet."

The lights exploded into twisting, spinning spirals. "Not stars. Fireworks! When did we get fireworks, Coach? They're so awesome!"

Tremblay got that sick I'm-not-going-to-tell-bad-news-to-Schreiber look. I had never seen it on an adult before—kids give me that look all the time, but not grown-ups. "Son, where exactly are these fireworks?"

"Right there." I pointed over the goalposts. "You can't miss them!" Strange, there were no booms or pops, just trails of silver, ripping across the night sky.

"Get me the EMT," Coach yelled to the trainer.

While my team went to get pizza, I went to the hospital.

"Scottie!" Ma yelled. She smothered me in breath-mint kisses. "I knew this would happen with all that football. All those bullies, always knocking you around, hurting my poor boy."

"Too hard," Pop mumbled.

"I didn't get hit too hard!" I yelled.

"Ma. She hugs too hard," Pop said.

"Oh, Scottie," Ma yelled louder, ignoring my father. "Does it hurt?" My mother never talked. She always shouted. Never in anger; she just liked to be sure people heard her. Pop, on the other hand, was quiet. He sniffled, blinked, and coughed when he wanted to say something. Once in a while, he'd even spout a word or two.

"He'll be fine." Dr. Faulkenham, a tall woman

with a quiet face came into the room. She had examined me when the ambulance brought me in.

"Oh, thank you for saving my baby," my mother gushed.

I wanted to climb into my bedpan. "Ma. Stop calling me your baby," I hissed.

Dr. Faulkenham laughed. "The tests are all clear. Scott's got lots of bumps and bruises but one must expect that on a football hero." She ripped opened the Velcro strap of my neck brace. "Up and at 'em."

I sat up, definitely sore but definitely fine.

"Football?" my father asked from the corner.

Dr. Faulkenham wrinkled her nose. "Excuse me?"

"My husband wants to know if Scottie can play football," Ma said.

Dr. Faulkenham's smile faded. "I don't know. What's this I hear about fireworks and shooting stars?" she asked, flashing a penlight into my eyes for the millionth time since I came in.

"Nothing," I lied. The light hurt but I kept my eyes open, toughing it out.

"Your coach said you claimed to see stars in the skies."

I laughed. "There *are* stars in the sky."

"Your coach didn't see them."

"No offense, but Coach Tremblay is old. Almost

fifty. His eyesight is going."

"Is he okay or ain't he?" my father asked.

"He appears to be fine, Mr. Schreiber." Dr. Faulkenham turned to me. "Even so, you probably shouldn't play football for a while."

"What!" I yelled. "Why not?"

"Just in case there's a slight head injury we're not picking up with the diagnostics."

"When can I play?" I moaned.

"Soon. Providing you have no headache and no other symptoms."

Ma crunched my fingers, trying to keep me from jumping down the lady's throat. "What symptoms?" my mother shouted. "What're you talking about!"

"You need to report anything out of the ordinary, Scott. Blurred vision, unsteadiness. Even a hearing disturbance or a strange taste in your mouth. Or"— she smiled—"too many stars in the sky."

Anything out of the ordinary. What about that daydream about flying during the football game? The screeching sounds? But hey, those happened before I got my bells rung in the end zone. Just crazy thoughts from hanging around with Mike Pillsbury, the weird-meister.

The heck with this—nothing was going to stop the Mighty Schreiber from going to the Super Bowl.

"Soon when? Like Monday. Right?" I asked.

"Soon . . . about a week," Dr. Faulkenham said.

12

"A week? No way!" I jumped off the stretcher. "I am so outta here!"

I ran out of the cubicle. As the stupid hospital gown flapped open, I flashed my butt at half the emergency department. I pulled the gown tighter, pretending that I strolled around bare-legged and bare-butted all the time. I was through the waiting room and almost to the exit when a squeaky voice stopped me.

"It's the Mighty Schreiber!" The Weird Band Girl jumped out of her chair and opened her arms. "He's okay!"

I booked it back to the emergency room. I didn't even care if my butt was hanging out. No way was any WBG going to get her hands on me.

Dr. Faulkenham made me a deal. If I had no symptoms, I could practice on Tuesday. That would give me three days to prepare for the Super Bowl. I swore on a stack of ear swabs that I would tell someone if my head went bonkers.

We celebrated the district title on Saturday with a monster bash at my house. As the guys came in, Pop shook all their hands. "Nice work," he muttered.

Ma hugged the guys with one arm while she shoved food at them with the other. "You boys need to eat," she shouted as she put out enough food to

13

sink a battleship: pizza with pepperoni and double cheese, sesame crackers and crab dip, peanut butter cookies with chocolate chips, foot-long hot dogs with chili, bacon burgers with melted Jarlsburg cheese, twenty kinds of soda, chocolate milk, and fruit juice.

Pop put videos of football bloopers on the wide-screen television. I vegged out in the recliner, day-dreaming of seeing my butt getting blooped in the NFL someday. DuCharme and Keras arm-wrestled at the dining room table. Clark farted in his armpit while Conner made his gut squeak. Hardy pushed straws up his nose and bet Monroe he could shoot soda out one side and milk out the other. Shattuck shoved cupcakes into his mouth, trying to break the team record of twelve. He gagged on number eleven, spewing yellow crumbs and pink frosting every-where.

Mike Pillsbury munched a plain hamburger and stared out the window. That kid spent too much time thinking. You name it, Pillsbury thinks it to death: math, science, history, even football and girls. And aliens, always aliens—up, down, left, right, morn-ing, noon, and night. Mike Pillsbury was obsessed with aliens. Too much *thinking* and not enough *doing* can make even the best kid a weirdo.

When the guys ran out to watch Shattuck puke on my front lawn, Pillsbury came over to me. "We need to talk, Scott."

14

"About what?" I said, munching a tortilla chip.

"Those stars," Pillsbury said. "The ones you saw over the goalpost."

I jumped up, scattering my chips. "Who said I saw stars?"

"You screamed at Coach to look at all the stars."

"I took a hard hit and I saw stars," I growled. "Want me to slap you silly so you can see how that works?"

"There's more, Scott."

"More of nothing is still nothing, you bozo."

"Your touchdown . . ." Pillsbury bit his lip and shuffled his feet.

"My touchdown won us a trip to the Super Bowl. Oh, sorry, I forgot to thank you." I made a deep bow and tipped my baseball cap. "A bazillion thanks for making a hole in the defensive line that only a toothpick or a phenomenal jock like me could slip through."

Pillsbury grabbed my arm. "There was so much going on, Scott. I don't think anyone else saw what really happened."

I yanked my arm away. "There was nothing to see except me winning the game for Ashby."

"Scott, you were almost to the goal line. Two Bristol tackles came in, one on each side. They missed you and collided with each other."

"And I just danced away from them and over the

goal line." I threw my hands up in the air. "Touchdown!"

"You didn't dance *away* from them," Pillsbury said. "You danced *over* them."

"So I went a little vertical."

"A little? Try three feet over their heads."

My gut caught fire. "Shut your face. I didn't jump over anyone's head. You're making stuff up again."

I headed for the door. The puke party had to be more fun than another Pillsbury cross-examination. Mike yanked me back. Most kids would get their lights beat out for a second illegal contact. But for old times sake, I let the kid live.

"Scott, it was like you flew over those two blockers. Five feet in the air at least. Flying—"

—I was flying as fast as my wings could take me. The Gargoyles shot mud balls from their snouts. One hit my wing and exploded into a fireball. My feathers flamed but I sang myself a song to dull the pain. I had to keep flying. If I couldn't fly—

"You are so full of crap! I can't fly." I shoved Pillsbury against the wall. "You and your crazy stories."

"Scott, listen to me . . ."

"No. You listen to me, Pillsbury. I hang out with you and I start seeing things and feeling things. Things I don't want to see and feel. Worse, I start

16

being afraid of things that don't even exist. You're turning me weird. I don't like it and I don't like having you for a friend. Just leave me alone."

Mike's eyes were spooky clear, as if he could see right through me. "Sure, I'll leave you alone, Scott. If that's what you want. But I can't guarantee that everyone else in the universe will."

3

THE GROUND RUSHED UP AT ME, A *mighty fist ready to whack me into tomorrow.*

It had happened in a flash. One moment I had wings. I flew over green trees, shining rivers, and misty mountains. Wind streams lifted me higher and higher until the world stretched below and I owned it all.

The next moment a blinding light sliced the sky. The air caught fire and I was tossed by crashing waves of heat and light. My eyes burned as I looked through a white-hot cloud of pain, trying to see what had ripped open my world.

One moment I flew. The next moment I fell.

And I kept falling.

I lifted my wings, trying to coast back into the air current. But they were gone!

In their place were arms and legs that I pumped like a fool on slick ice—a fool with nowhere to go but down. Just as the ground slammed me into a million pieces, I screamed out my last words.

"Pillsbury, I'm gonna kill you!"

I was flat on my back, frozen to the hard ground. Nick Thorpe looked down at me from the tree house. "Hey, you guys oughta see this!" he choked. "The Mighty Schreiber"—*snort, snort*—"sacked himself!"

Cripes, I could take Thorpe's smart mouth but that constant snorting drove me bonkers. Why didn't that kid's parents take him to a nose doctor before I stuck my fist through his tonsils?

Pillsbury hustled his skinny butt down the ladder. "You okay, Scott?"

"Gimme a minute." My head killed but that was from Friday's game. The rest of me felt fine—a hundred bumps and bruises, but that was normal after any big game. "Why wouldn't I be okay?"

Pillsbury blinked, shuffled, glanced at the sky. He had that I'm-not-gonna-tell-bad-news-to-Scott-Schreiber look I see a lot on kids.

"Spit it out, doofball," I growled.

"Um. How's your head? After that injury and all."

"Duh. Clean your glasses, moron. It's right here, still on my shoulders."

"I meant . . . the stuff inside your head. Your brain . . . you thinking clearly?"

"You wanna die now or later, Pillsbury? Why are you asking me such a stupid question?"

"Scott, you just launched yourself out of the tree house. As if you were trying to fly!"

The mighty fist whacked me again. *One moment I had wings* . . . and then what? My head felt like the inside of a cotton candy machine, all hazy and puffy, spinning in circles.

Was I getting as weird as Mike Pillsbury?

"Why did you make me send everyone home?" Pillsbury asked five minutes later.

"I'm not spilling my guts to Thorpe and your other wacko friends," I said. "If I'm going nuts, I don't need the whole world to know about it."

"Because you fell out of a tree house?"

"Because I flew. I flew out of the tree house and over a forest. Following a river that glowed like diamonds. Over mountains that were peaked with snow. Into a deep blue sky where the stars—"

"Scott!" Pillsbury's green eyes shone like a cat about to pounce.

"What!" I sat cross-legged on the old, flat pillow that I had dug out of my garage and brought to the tree house.

Pillsbury pointed. "That's what," he whispered.

There were two inches of empty space between my butt and the pillow.

"Holy crap!" I leaped for the door. Pillsbury tackled me. We went down hard. Pillsbury's breath smelled like chocolate and his arms around my knees were surprisingly strong.

"Let me go!"

"Promise you won't fly out of the tree house again," he said.

"I gotta get out of here!" I panted.

"Swear you won't fly!" Mike yelped, squeezing tighter.

"Swear." I gulped. "I hope."

We sat up. "It's happening again. Just like at the game," Mike said. "How're you doing it?"

"I dunno. Maybe we're both just seeing things?"

"Maybe," Pillsbury said. "Mass hysteria, they call it, when two or more people go nuts together. We should just forget it."

Forget it. Forget Mike Pillsbury and his crazy stories of aliens and weird worlds and star travel. Forget that any of Pillsbury's ravings had ever happened. We had been warned the aliens never would, never *could* come again. So Mike was right. I couldn't fly. And aliens could only be found in good stories and bad dreams.

Chalk it up to mass hysteria and just forget it. Forget it and go home. Go to bed, go to school, go to football, get away from Pillsbury. Let my life shade back to black and white. Probably the smartest thing to do. But then I thought: black and white equals gray. And gray equals boring.

"The story you told," I said. "Tell it again, just for me."

4

iF YoU LiSTEN CAREFULLY, YoU CAN
hear the music of the stars.

Stand in the darkness, listen in the stillness, hold your gaze on the stars, and you'll hear the music that stretches across infinity, that binds every possibility into a wonderful certainty.

The music of the stars is said to come from the Lyras, one of the most ancient races of the universe. When the Bom were still a lawless folk and Earthlings huddled in caves, the Lyras were an advanced race, beings gifted with intelligence, wisdom, and imagination. The Lyras scattered from their home system eons ago to become wandering minstrels among the stars. Esteemed as elder statesmen, they were devoted to filling the universe with song and serenity. Today there are not many people *left who remember the Lyras, or even believe in them.*

The universe was taken over by younger races, cruel and violent, that fought against everything the Lyras sang for. There were the Mantix, creatures of low intelligence and brutal slime that work for the highest bidder. The Jong we already know—collectors and oppressors of all thinking beings. And worst of them all—the Shard, a people of sharp skin and vile minds who spread outward from the constellation of Pavo like a plague.

For as long as anyone can remember, the Shards have been at war. They roared through the galaxy like a wildfire roars through a dry forest, destroying everything in its path. At this time, they were fighting the Ursas, gentle bear-like folk from Ursa Minor. The Ursas had an asteroid belt rich in boron, an element that the Shards needed to run their starships. The Ursas would have been happy to enter a trade agreement but the Shards never thought to ask.

They just came and took.

A war of surprising ferocity started. The Shards never expected the Ursas to be so determined in protecting their own space. The conflict lingered until the Shards exhausted all their weapons. They were faced with the unthinkable—surrender—when someone discovered an ancient microchip telling the legend of the Lyras.

The Shards learned that the song of a Lyra has the power to persuade—to calm a fire-breathing Pyrolite to sweet slumber or to rally a timid Mystic to vicious war. The Shards reasoned that if they could find a Lyra and enslave it, they would have a formidable weapon against the Ursas. The song of a Lyra in the cutting hands of the Shards would be the most dangerous force in the universe.

Vowing to find a Lyra, the Shards embarked on a quest that has stretched across time, across space— a quest that continues today.

Look in the sky before dawn, when the moon has set but the sun still sleeps. Look for that flash, that twinkle of light. That's a sign the Shards are out there searching. They won't stop until they find what they want.

And they won't let anyone—Bom, Sirian, or Earthling—get in their way.

"Stop it!" I grabbed Pillsbury's jacket and yanked him up. His skinny shoulders hunched around his ears but his face stayed calm. Pillsbury wasn't afraid of me, not anymore. But I was beginning to fear myself. "Tell me it's not true," I gasped.

Pillsbury wiggled away. "No one makes you come here, Scott. The Chronicles are stories. Take them for what they are. Even if one of them happened to come true, we just have to forget that. We were warned—"

Pillsbury shuddered and I shuddered with him,

remembering the brutal attack of the Jong just a few weeks ago. Sometimes it seemed so unreal, like it had never happened. But sometimes I woke in a sweat, seeing those poisonous fangs ready to sack me into forever.

"The Chronicles are mostly stories. Take them or leave them. Why should I care?" He shrugged his arms back into his jacket, swung over the ladder, and disappeared into his yard. Moments later, a door slammed.

I was alone in Mike's tree house. It wasn't even supper time but the sky was dark with the early night that comes in November. The first stars blinked on the horizon. A blast of frigid air hit me, bringing a hint of ice and the smell of winter. For a moment, there were crystals in the air. Maybe it would snow. I loved playing football in the snow.

The crystals were gone as quickly as they came, scattered by the wind. Stars over the end zone, crystals in the night air? Was I brain-damaged? Or were more aliens about to swarm into my life? The hairs on the back of my neck rose like tiny soldiers.

Stop it, Schreiber. Pillsbury doesn't have to make you nuts—you're making yourself psycho. I swung out of the tree house and dropped to solid ground, stomping my feet to make sure I stayed there. I was done listening to Mike Pillsbury and his crazy Chronicles.

No more aliens for me.

5

THE SHARD GLIMMERED LIKE ALU-

*minum foil. His eyes were crystal tunnels, flashing
with silver before disappearing into empty sockets.
His hair was like a million needles, harmless-looking
in neat rows, but I wouldn't want to be this guy's
barber. His fingers were long and smooth, tipped
with claws as sharp as knife blades.*

*His hands circled my throat. I panted with fear,
and though I willed my feet to stay firm, I swayed.
Blood trickled, hot on my neck, then cooling as it
worked its way between my shoulder blades.*

*I jammed my hands into the Shard's windpipe.
Sparks flew from his brittle skin but he didn't
make a sound; he just choked me harder. Tiny needles, like a swarm of tiny wasps, pricked my
skin. The trickle of blood turned to a steady stream*

and the night became a red haze.

Fly! Even if he holds on, so what? Fly so high that he'll run out of air and let go. And even if he doesn't give up, fly so high that when he slashes the life out of you, he'll drop to the ground with you and shatter to a million pieces.

FLY, you goose-bellied, Bom-faced, son-of-a-Loapher! FLY!

And I flew.

Bam! Right into the underside of my top bunk. The Shard was gone, a bad dream crumbling into night dust. Nothing to be scared of, I told myself. Until I realized—

—I floated two feet over my mattress. Only the top bunk had stopped me from going higher.

One moment I was dying. The next moment I was flying. Then I was in the bathroom, puking so hard that even dying looked like fun.

"Scott?" Pop called out.

"Ugh," I said, spitting out re-stewed hot dogs and beans.

My father grumbled. "The boy's sick."

"My baby!" Ma gushed.

Within seconds, she was slopping cold water on my face and rubbing my head so hard I thought my hair would fall out. Her eyes were half closed but her voice was wide-awake. "Is it your head, Scottie?" she boomed. "The doctor said to watch out for your head."

"Ma, I'm okay. I just ate too much supper. I'm all right now."

"Let me tuck you back in."

"No!" I yelled. I shoved her out the door.

"Are you sure?"

"Yes!" I yelled.

Ma turned back and grabbed me in a bear hug. "I knew you needed tucking."

"No!" I yelled. "I don't want to be tucked in. Yes, I am okay!"

"Okay?" Pop called.

"Okay!" Ma and I yelled at the same time. Now even the neighbors down the street knew I was okay.

I washed my face, the sink, my mouth over and over, then dragged myself back to my room. I ripped the blanket and sheets off my bottom bunk, half afraid that I would find puddles of blood. Nothing. Just a bad, stupid dream. But no way I was getting back into that bed. I didn't know which was worse: the Shard leaning over me or the bedsprings whacking my face. A nasty, double-decker nightmare. I dragged my blanket and pillow to the floor. I wrapped up, shut my eyes, and . . .

. . . *the Shard and the Jong raged at each other, the flashing hands of the Shard and the venom of the Jong whipping up a storm of foaming poison. Then they saw me. The Jong flicked that cobra tongue and the Shard beamed like a thousand suns.*

Why waste each other when they had a perfectly good Earthling to annihilate?

I jolted myself awake and stared at the ceiling. The plaster was flaked, dented from all my practice passes. Even a foam football can do considerable damage in the hands of a master.

Football, that's it. Focus, Schreiber. Review the game plan. The field stretched out like my own private playground; my players were soldiers I could move at will. I bent down behind my center, checked my front line, then barked out the signals. *Snap!* The ball was in my hands.

I stepped out, cocked my arm for the pass, faked a look downfield at my decoys. Ashby scarlet, one cutting midfield, one ranging deep, took the enemy's defense out for a picnic while I marked time for my real receiver to swing behind me. *One two three, turn, and hand off.* The ball snug in my running back's belly, he followed his blocker into enemy territory. I ran behind him, covering his back, that shimmering red Ashby shirt that declared number thirty-three and the name— *Pillsbury?* I gave the ball to Mike Pillsbury? To the master klutz?

A Bristol beetle, radiating waves of garlic, bombed in on Mike's flank. "Watch it!" I yelled. But it was too late. The Bristol player stomped Pillsbury underfoot, grinding him into hot dog puke. Then the thug turned toward me. His shiny snout dripped acid through the bars of his helmet.

"Gargoyle!" I screamed and leaped over the goalposts. I leaped again and jammed my face into the scoreboard, forty feet above the field. The flashing red letters were bigger than Montana.

ALIENS: INFINITY

MIGHTY SCHREIBER: ZERO

I woke up and hugged the cold floor, grateful to still be in contact with solid ground—even if it was covered with dust bunnies and gum wrappers. But I was desperate to get some rest. I had to stay fresh for Friday's Super Bowl. How was I ever going to get some real sleep?

Homework.

I dragged out my battered notebook, stuffed with assignments, football plays, and love notes from half the girls in seventh grade. I wiped my eyes, trying to get a good look at tomorrow's—ugh, today's—science assignment. What the heck? I almost rubbed my eyes into mush, not believing what I was seeing. My death sentence was written in big black letters across the worksheet:

SCIENCE PROJECT, DUE NOVEMBER 19, 10:30A.M.

Today was Monday, November 19. The time was 1:30 A.M. The science project was due in nine hours.

31

The science project assigned in September that would be half our grade for this term. The science project that could get me bounced off the football team if I didn't pass it in.

The science project that I had totally blown off.

All fall, I had thought there was plenty of time to get this science thing in gear. But as my clock ticked to 1:31, then 1:32, time was running out. It was too late to run to the library, dash to a hobby store, grow some flowers, dig some roots, pin some bugs, or— when all else failed, beg Uncle Burt for one of his pickled frogs. With only a few hours left, I only had one option play to call.

And his name was Mike Pillsbury.

6

"**TELL ME AGAIN WHAT WE'RE DOING** out here," Pillsbury whined.

"Here" was Willard Forest—home to the state's tallest pine trees, densest brush, and fastest streams. And, I hoped, home to something that would pass as my science project.

An hour earlier, I had used the key under the welcome mat to get into the Pillsbury house. "Don't eat my brain!" Mike yelped as I shook him out of sleep. Pillsbury was always paranoid about some alien eating his brain. Like they don't have better things to eat in outer space.

He glared through gunk-crusted eyes. "I thought we weren't friends anymore."

"Yeah, well I was just kidding." I grinned. "You *can* take a joke—right, Pillsbury?"

"Ha ha." He yawned and rolled over, trying to go back to sleep. I bounced him out of bed and muscled him into the bathroom.

"Hurry up," I nagged as he brushed his teeth for five minutes straight. He combed his hair, climbed into thermal underwear, flannel-lined jeans, and rubber boots. He put on a warm coat, a hat with earflaps, and thermal mittens. Then we biked three miles to the deepest woods in this part of the state.

"Answer my question. Why Willard Forest?"

Dark trees and darker night surrounded us, making Willard Forest one of those black holes Pillsbury blabbers about. The moon rose over the barren trees, giving just enough light to throw dagger-shaped shadows. The woods were silent, the only sounds my feet crackling in the dry leaves and Pillsbury tripping every three steps. In the daylight, the main paths of the forest were broad and clear, like dirt highways through a long-gone world. But in the middle of this November night, our flashlights bounced on the path like shaky candles.

I felt very small.

"Anytime you want to give me an answer, Scott."

"I told you—I need something to turn in for my science project."

"Let me rephrase the question," Pillsbury said. "How could you be so *stupid* that you forgot your science project?"

How could you *be stupid enough to iron creases into your jeans?* I wanted to shout. *How could* you *be stupid enough to answer all the questions before the teachers even ask them, not leaving anything for the rest of us? How could* you *be stupid enough to tell girls about parsecs and quasars when they want to hear about their nice smiles and cool clothes and pretty eyes?*

But I bit my tongue. Now wasn't the time to inform the genius of his own stupidity. "I got busy," I said, ducking a branch.

"You got busy!" he hollered. "Yow!" Same branch—Pillsbury walked into it. "I finished my science project three weeks ago."

"Shut up. Besides, it's all your fault."

"My fault? Why is it my fault?"

"Remember Halloween?" I said.

"Shh!" Mike said. "We're not supposed to talk about that!"

"Tough. You dragged me out of my bed and into a spaceship!"

That wasn't exactly true. Pillsbury did drag me out of bed and into a spaceship, but I hadn't really been minding my own business. Right before Halloween, when we were still enemies, I had played a trick on Pillsbury at a dance. He freaked out and, because he sometimes thinks he might be an alien, he sent out an SOS through his satellite dish to outer space.

Much to his surprise, help came. So did a bunch of other creatures that weren't so helpful, like the evil Jong, the disgusting Mantix, and the slimy Bom. It took Mike, our friend Katelyn, me, and a poodlelike Sirian named Barnabus to get all those aliens to go home again.

"Well, now you've dragged me out of bed, we're even," Pillsbury said. "So what is it you're looking for?"

"I don't know," I said.

"You don't know. Figures."

The cold seeped through my football jacket. My hands shook, making the flashlight beam shudder on the prickly brush. Dried branches scratched my face as I pushed off the main path. We had to get deeper into the woods. Anything cool enough to qualify for a science project wouldn't be just lying around where all the hikers, mountain-bikers, and birders hung out.

A light flashed in the sky. *The Shard*, I thought, falling back into my nightmare. *He wants to finish what he started.* I jogged a few feet, trying to outrun the chills. *Come on, focus! Even though it's the middle of a November night and I'm hanging out in a deep, dark forest, I'm safe.*

Safe.

Except that Pillsbury was no longer behind me. I flicked my flashlight around on the brush, the shadows bending into a thousand shapes. No Albert Michael Pillsbury. I opened my mouth to holler but then snapped it shut before any sound leaked out. Whatever got Mike could find me. I didn't want to be a jerk, but hey—they always eat the kids with the brains. The kids with muscles, they leave alone.

I hoped.

I stood still. Concentrating. Listening. No twigs breaking. No brush rustling. No Pillsbury complaining. Nothing. Wait, maybe there was something. No, that was just a little wind in the pines. Was something behind me? No, just dark. Dark and silence. It was almost nice to be alone. The moon was above the trees now, full and rich. The stars were a million eyes, winking with secrets. The sky was a deep blue cup that never ran empty.

Why Willard Forest, Pillsbury had wanted to know. What had I been thinking? Then I realized, I hadn't been *thinking* anything. I just *knew* we had to come here. Something had drawn me here, something I couldn't hear or see. But, just as I knew where my receiver would be when I was ready to unload a pass, I knew something waited for me.

I closed my eyes and listened deeper. My mind ached like a balloon that stretches thin with too much air. I couldn't hold all the—the what? What was I hearing? Not words. Not thoughts, pictures, ideas. What I heard was—

Certainty.

Certainty ran over me, filling my imagination, moving the soul I never even thought about having.

The music of the stars.

7

i COULD HAVE LiSTENED FOREVER. BUT

as I soaked in the music, a crackling noise leaked in around the edges. Something moved over the hard, cold ground. *Snap-pad-snap*—ragged footsteps broke the rhythm of the star song.

I turned to look. Then the night exploded around me. I ripped through the underbrush back to the main path where Pillsbury stood like a post, staring at the sky.

"Bear!" I bellowed.

"Are you nuts?" Pillsbury yelped as I trampled him. I yanked him off the ground and turned his head in the right direction. His eyes went wide.

"Bear!" he yelled, racing ahead of me. Jeepers, why can't that kid run like that on the football field?

The bear panted and *womfed* from the darkness,

as if the dumb beast was having a heart attack. But it kept coming. Two hours earlier I had been in a stupid dream, terrified of a Shard's claws at my neck. Now I had a real bear nipping at my real butt. Gaining—thirty feet behind, now twenty, and now closing.

Bam! Pillsbury skidded to a stop. I crashed into him. Ahead of us was a wall of briars. Dead end. Behind us, a *womfing* beast ready to leap down our throats. Deader end.

"Jump!" I yelled. We jumped at the same time, into the same tree.

"Bears can climb trees!" Pillsbury panted as he scrambled up ahead of me.

"You got a better idea?" I pushed his backside out of my face so we could move faster. "Besides, this is a wimp tree, too small for a bear to climb."

And too small for two football players to climb, even if one of us was a scrawny geek. When we reached the top of the tree, its skinny branches wimped out under our weight.

"Don't move!" I hissed to Pillsbury as the top of the tree arched toward the ground.

No problem—Pillsbury was frozen to a thin branch, eyes squeezed shut, face pasty white in the moonlight.

A lifetime later, I looked down. My heart hammered in my chest, trying to punch its way out.

Though the sky grew gray with dawn, the brush under us was still a mass of shadows. But no sign of the bear.

Pillsbury finally opened his eyes. "Good one, Schreiber."

"How was I supposed to know there were bears in these woods?" I snapped.

"Woods? Bears? They do go together. But then again, you don't pay much attention in science class, do you?" Pillsbury shifted on his branch and the whole tree shuddered. "Where is it?"

"I think it just kept going." I swung my feet up and straddled the limb. The tree shuddered under my weight. "Maybe it wasn't even after us."

"What else could the bear have been after?" Pillsbury growled. "Who or what else is insane enough to be running around in the woods at night? Except you—and me, who was stupid enough to follow you here."

"Shut up, Pillsbury," I said. "Why do you always have to be right and everyone else wrong?"

My life was falling apart. My awesome football career was about to go up in smoke because I forgot my science project, I got chased by a bear, and—worst of all—I was getting weird. Lights in the sky. Music in the stars. What kind of drooling maniac was I turning into?

"So what do we do now?" Pillsbury asked. "Sit

here until the forest rangers rescue us? We could be facing frostbite. Dehydration. Exposure."

"Close that stinkin' mouth before I jam my fist down it!" I roared. "I gotta think!"

Pillsbury snorted. "Think? *Think?* That's revolutionary, Schreiber."

I stared into the sky, trying to focus. The mountains in the distance were dabbed with pink and gold. One star blinked overhead but it didn't have long before daylight would knock it out of the sky.

No padding steps, no panting, no brush bending, no *womfing*. Even the icy breeze had died away. How long should we stay in the tree to be sure the bear was really gone? How long would it be before Ma called me for breakfast and found me missing? How long before Mr. FitzPatrick flunked me and I got kicked out of football?

I was counting up the how-longs when the sky exploded.

"Holy sugar!" I jumped up. "There they are again!" The horizon was filled with glittering lights, as if someone had tossed stardust into the wind.

"What the heck?" Pillsbury stood up. *Crack!* His branch broke. He grabbed me, trying to save himself. As we crashed to the ground, I had only one thought.

Why can't I fly when I really need to?

* * *

"I'm going to be picking pinecones out of my butt for days," I moaned.

"Quiet." Pillsbury scurried up onto a rock. The sky was a clear blue-gray, ready for morning. The lights were gone.

"I told you I saw stars," I said.

"You swore you didn't!" Pillsbury snapped.

"Well, now you saw them too. So if I'm crazy, I'm only as crazy as you are, Pillsbury. Cripes, that's pretty crazy."

"Hey, I'm not the one who flew out of the tree house," he muttered.

"Well, we can't all be perfect like you." I climbed the rock with him. "What do you think they were?"

"I don't know. Couldn't be the aurora borealis. We're too far south."

"What's the roaring boring whatever?" I asked.

"Aurora borealis," Pillsbury said in his I'm-smarter-than-the-rest-of-the-world tone. "The northern lights, usually visible at the North Pole. A shining display of particles in the upper atmosphere."

"Yeah, well," I said. "We're not near the North Pole."

Pillsbury climbed off the rock. "But you did see them, right?"

Yeah, I saw lights and I ran from a bear and I heard the stars sing and I flew into my top bunk. Life was as weird as it could get. "A lotta good it'll do me. It's not like I can say, 'This is my science project, Mr. FitzPatrick. I saw UFOs in the sky.'"

The thought struck me like a lightning bolt. "Pillsbury! Maybe they came back!"

"They can't," Mike said. "Earth is off-limits. You know that."

"But maybe they don't know that," I said. "Maybe they're here to . . . to . . ." I stopped, having reached the limit of my imagination. Pillsbury was the storyteller, not me.

"Admit it, Schreiber. You got yourself in trouble and no one from the stars is coming to rescue you."

"That stupid science project!" I yelled, and kicked the broken tree. The flaking bark crumbled under my foot. "Stupid, stupid," I said, and kept kicking. The wood cracked. It felt good doing damage to something, even if it was a poor little tree. Kick, stupid, kick, stupid.

Then I saw it, shining in the guts of the busted tree. Gold, silver, and purple strands laced through field hay and faded grass. The most amazing bird's nest.

I pulled it out, gently. Then I realized I didn't have to be so careful. The nest was woven solidly with strands that acted like a frame, holding the straw and grass as firmly as nails hold wood. "They're like metal," I said.

"They *are* metal," Pillsbury replied in his professor's voice. "Some birds will scavenge for cloth, paper, or string to use as building materials. But I never heard of a bird that would use metal. How could a bird shape it so easily?"

My heart hammered again, this time with excitement. This was a treasure, something that perhaps no other human had ever seen, not if these birds made a habit of hiding their nests inside trees. "It's awesome."

"It is," Pillsbury agreed. "But where are the birds?"

"It's November," I said. "They've gone south."

"I suppose. But . . ."

"But what?"

"This nest seems built to last out centuries, let alone a simple winter," Pillsbury answered. "Maybe we should just leave it here where . . ."

But I was already walking away, the nest cradled against my ribs like a football.

"Where you going?" Pillsbury shouted.

"Home," I said. "I've found my science project."

8

i'M WALKiNG oN AiR, i THoUGHT.
High as a kite. Flying.

Flying?

I glanced down, relieved to see my feet still touching the scuffed floor tiles of Ashby Middle School. The heck with Pillsbury's stories, my bad dreams, and flashing stars. This was real and this was awesome. I was a hero and everyone knew it.

The guys swarmed me. "Schreiber, ready to roast Super Bowl turkey?"

"Way to go, thirteen."

"Hey, man. Cool game."

The teachers respected me. "Scott, nice job Friday night."

"Glad your head's okay."

"Great comeback in the last quarter."

The girls adored me. Beth ran her orange finger-nails through my hair. "Is this where that Bristol jerk hit you?" she purred.

Nicole squeezed my biceps. "I knew they wouldn't stop you, Scottie. You're too strong."

Kayleigh smiled as she slipped me a note. "My phone number," she said. "In case you want to talk football . . . or other contact sports."

Christmas, my birthday, and Halloween put together could never be as sweet as this Monday morning. And to make the day perfect, my nest was carefully packed in a box, ready for science class.

Walking on air beat flying in nightmares any day.

"Hey, want to see something cool?" I asked the crowd of girls. I slid the nest out of the box. "Isn't it great?"

The strands of the nest sparkled in the overhead lights. Gold and silver reflected on E.J.'s face. "I don't get what's so great about it," she said.

"Whattya mean?" I sputtered.

"It's not a grand palace," I said.

"What would I want with a palace when I could have our children?" she hummed.

We carried the nest between us as we rose through the limbs of the Harna tree. The broad leaves rippled with purple coolness. We fluttered through, singing: "Woven from sunlight and moon-

beams. Cast forever in the shape of our love."

"It's just a bag of old grass," E.J. said.

"Huh?" I said, shaking my head to clear the haze. "What did you say?"

"Forget it." E.J. slipped away. The other girls pushed closer.

"You think it's cool, don't you?" I asked Nicole.

Nicole shrugged. "It's okay."

Beth shoved her out of the way. "I like it, Scott. It's really special."

"Yeah, isn't it?" I pushed her fingers against the nest. "Here, touch the strands, see how cool they are. Actually they're warm—which makes them cool."

Beth yanked her hand away. "Thanks, Scott." She wiped her hand on her jeans.

"Look how it sparkles." I lifted it to her face.

"Your song in my ears, cast forever in our love . . ."

"Scott, no offense, but it's kind of dirty," she said.

"Dirty?"

"And smelly," Kayleigh chimed in.

Were they blind? Or just stupid? No, I was the stupid one, expecting dumb girls to appreciate nature. "Hey, it's been in the woods. But look at it! How could you not see that it's . . . it's . . ."

"It's what, Scott?" Kayleigh asked.

"It's . . . it's . . ." There was only one word that fit. "It's beautiful."

Beth slapped her hands over her mouth, stifling

48

laughter. My stomach flip-flopped. How had such a shocking word come out of my mouth? Beth glanced at Kayleigh and all the girls exploded.

"Get lost, you slime bats!" I growled.

The warning bell rang and the girls headed for their lockers. "Thanks for sharing," Nicole called. Beth sputtered with giggles as they scurried down the hall.

I yanked open my locker, almost twisting the door off.

"Now that your fan club is gone, can I touch your"—*snort*—"nest?"

"Shut up, Thorpe," I mumbled.

"But it's such a nice nest," he whined. "Bee-yoo-tee-full."

"You want me to shut you up?"

"I want a nest just like yours so all the girls will worship me, too."

I counted to ten, dragged out my books, and slammed the door.

Thorpe flittered around me like a pesky horsefly. "Look everyone, look what I found in the woods! Uh, maybe it has some pretty feathers in it. Football heroes love pretty things."

"I'm warning you, Thorpe."

"Or if we're really lucky, maybe we'll find . . . ta-da! . . . bird poop." His snorts machine-gunned out of his nose. "Bee-yoo-tee-full birdie poop.

The chicks love that stuff!"

The kid just wouldn't stop. Until I put my fist into his face.

Thorpe, ice pack to his face, waited for his mother to pick him up at the nurse's office. He was suspended for fighting. I only got an in-house detention. "Why did you do it?" I asked. "Why did you tell Goodrich you hit me first?"

Nick took the ice away from his nose. It was swollen and red but it had stopped bleeding. "You're a jerk, Schreiber. Can't take a joke, never could."

"And you can't keep your flappin' mouth shut. But that doesn't explain why you took the blame."

Thorpe closed his eyes, leaned his head back, and rested the ice on his forehead. "If you got suspended for fighting, you might be off the team."

I had never thought of that. When I punched Nick, all I could think of was defending my nest.

The bombs exploded around us—balls of acid, regurgitated from the Gargoyles. "The nest," she cried, and I dove through the flames, my wings flat, not fearing the ground or the Gargoyles or the Shards.

I feared only that my children would never see sunlight and moonbeams.

"What did you say, Thorpe?" I said, confused. Another dream? I must have dozed off for a second;

staying up all night, chasing shadows, and being chased by bears can do that to a guy.

"I said, 'A kid like you can never lose. And a kid like me can never win.'"

My throat closed and I had to swallow hard to breathe. I was the lowest kind of scum, letting a jerk like Nick provoke me and then take the blame. Football or not, I couldn't let this idiot be a better man than me. "It's my fault. I'll go tell Goodrich the truth."

"No way."

"Why should I let a zero like you get in trouble for me?"

"If you get suspended for hitting me, everyone will still blame me for getting you kicked off the team. For the rest of my life, I'll be the kid who made Ashby lose its first Super Bowl without even stepping on the field."

Nick took the ice off his face and grinned crookedly; the left side of his face was swelling. "But if I get suspended for hitting you first, well . . . you get to play football. And I go down in Ashby history as the only kid who ever dared to pick on Scott Schreiber. That way, everyone wins."

So why did I feel like such a loser?

9

i DRAGGED ALONG LiKE A DOG WHO has been caught with his nose in the trash. My head hung low; if I had had a tail, it would have curled miserably between my legs. On the way to second period class, kids waved, smiled, slapped my back. To them, I was still the Mighty Schreiber, football hero.

Inside, I was just Scott Schreiber, Thorpe-bashing creep.

I stopped a dozen times, ready to go back and confess to Principal Goodrich. But Nick was right; no matter what happened, he'd get blamed. This way he got to look like a big shot instead of a mouse turd.

I was almost to math class when the screech slammed me against the wall. I staggered, trying to stay on my feet. Pain cut through my head like a hot poker. Kids walked by, laughing, joking, arguing. No one else seemed to hear it.

Was my skull turning itself inside out? Dr. Faulkenham had mentioned strange symptoms. I ground my hands into my ears but the screech wouldn't stop. The spit curdled in my mouth. Somehow among the shrieking sirens I remembered how I'd made it go away last Friday.

The Weird Band Girl.

I lurched down the eighth-grade hall. The older kids looked at me, surprised to see a seventh grader in this part of the school. "Hi, Scott," a girl said. "You okay? Looks like your head hurts."

"A little," I mumbled. "But I'm okay."

"Hey, Schreiber!" Crisostamo punched my arm. "What're you doing at this end of the building? Trolling for older women?"

"The band room," I spat through my clenched teeth.

"The band room? Are you psycho? You ever see what kind of woofers come out of that place?"

I grabbed Crisostamo's shirt and hoisted him toward the lights. "The band room, man!"

"Whatever rings your chimes, thirteen." Crisostamo steered me down a narrow hall to the part of the school reserved for kids with no lives. Industrial Arts. Agricultural Studies. Domestic Sciences.

Band.

I whipped the door open. The music roared over me and I rumbled like a volcano ready to blow its top. "Stop!" I yelled. "Stop it now!"

The teacher, who was conducting, dropped her arms and stared in amazement. Slowly, the kids lowered their instruments or quieted their drums, confusion in their faces as the music died.

First a creep and now a fool. Another record-setting day for Scott Schreiber. But at least the screech stopped.

I grinned and waved. "Just wanted to thank you for the great job Friday night!" I clapped and everyone joined me. While we applauded each other, I scanned the band bonks, looking for the WBG. Taped glasses, orange lipstick, teased hair, striped shirts with checked trousers—there's no geek circus bigger than band practice. Except maybe Pillsbury's computer club.

I spotted the Weird Band Girl in the front row, sitting right under the conductor's stand. I pointed at her. "Um . . . Mr. Goodrich wants to see . . . um, what's-her-name there."

"How do you know it's me Mr. Goodrich wants if you don't know my name?" She glared at me. The band bonks laughed. I shot them a dirty look that silenced every last one of them.

"It's okay," the teacher said. "Go with Scott."

The Weird Band Girl followed me into the hall, glaring daggers with every step.

"Well, aren't you about as stupid as a kid can get and still walk upright!" the WBG sneered. "Barging in like that, making a donkey of yourself."

A band bozo calling me—Ashby's finest—stupid? I was almost speechless. "I thought . . ."

"You thought what?" she snapped.

"I thought . . . you, you know . . ."

"I know a lot, but I don't know what you're pretending to be thinking. If you actually do think."

"You came to the hospital and everything," I blurted. "I thought you . . . were worried about me."

"You fool," she snarled. "They *made* us go and show support. I was happy to see you were okay because that meant we got to go home!"

"Oh," I said. And stupidly, repeated it. "Oh." I blinked my eyes from embarrassment; she blinked hers because . . . well, she's a blinker.

She broke the silence. "I suppose you're here to tell me how terrible my playing sounds."

Inside the band room, the music had resumed. No screeching or strangled sirens, just your run-of-the-mill school spirit stuff. There was no doubt about it; the Weird Band Girl was the culprit.

"Look," I said, "it's probably not your fault. I had some sort of stupid head injury and for some reason, when you play, I . . . I . . ."

The silence was as hard as steel—until the WBG broke it. "You die?" she whispered.

"I only wish I could die, it's so bad," I whispered back, waiting for her to slap me. But instead her face burst with tears—a downpour like those summer thundershowers when the clouds are dark and heavy and the rain pelts in huge drops.

I had been a creep and a fool already today; I wasn't about to be a scumbag. I had no choice but to pat her back and say nice things.

Even if it meant touching a Weird Band Girl.

When she stopped blubbering, the Weird Band Girl took me to a room at the back of the school so we could talk. "My private study room," she said.

"What the heck! How do you rate your own room? All I have is a grungy book locker and a grungier gym locker."

The WBG unlocked the door. Inside was a piano, a rack of instruments, two music stands. Posters filled the wall: *Appearing in London. New York. Tokyo. Los Angeles. Paris.* "You don't know who I am, do you?" she asked.

"Uh . . ." Her face smiled from every wall. Stacia Caraviello, the posters called her. She was famous. Not just Ashby-famous, like me. The Weird Band Girl was *world*-famous.

"I don't blame you for not knowing," she said. "I

didn't know who you were either."

"What the heck? You do all this but you play in the stupid school band?"

"It's not stupid. Just amateurish. I do it for fun and to play different instruments. In fact, I came to Ashby Middle School this year just for fun. I got sick of tutors and traveling. I wanted to do something normal."

"What do you play?" I asked. "That thing with the cigar mouthpiece?"

"That's an oboe, dum—" She snipped off the insult. "An oboe. Normally you wouldn't play that in marching band, but last Friday my trumpet, sax, and flute all were making that—you know—that—"

Yeah, I knew that sinus-splitting nightmare that she called music.

"In concert, I perform the violin. I've been playing since I was two. But now even my violin has turned on me. Every time I draw the bow, it's agony."

"I don't get it. If you're so good," I said, "how come you sound like—like—"

"Like fingers on a chalkboard?" She pouted.

"Like a cat getting its tail amputated?"

She tilted her head, a half smile showing through her tears. "Like a devil with a sunburn?"

"Like a slippery hog in a spinning blender?" I upped her.

"Like buzzards dancing on high-voltage lines?" She smiled.

"Like my singing?" I tra-la-la-ed. She stared at me like I was nuts. I yodeled. Her eyes stopped blinking and started sparkling.

"I can't be *that* bad!" Stacia plopped onto the piano bench. "Nothing could be that bad!" Laughing, she leaned back onto the keyboard.

Screech!

"The piano, too?" she gasped, her eyes blinking with disbelief. "Even a mindless rodent can make a decent sound on a piano!" She reached for another key. Her fingers were long and delicate. *Screech!* And deadly.

She grabbed her ears and bolted to the other side of the room. "You try it," Stacia said.

"It's not my problem," I snapped, my head still echoing with pain.

"Do it!"

I punched the keyboard. We both grabbed our ears as the screech bounced from wall to wall.

"It's you, too." Stacia grabbed a drumstick and a wooden block. "Let's try an experiment," she said, handing me the drumstick. "Tap this."

"No way."

"You said it wasn't you. So what are you afraid of?"

Nothing, except watching the gray matter leak out of my ears when my brain melted. I gently touched the drumstick to the wood. *Screech!*

I backed into a music stand, knocking it over onto a trombone. The clatter and clanging was a relief after the screeching.

"It's both of us," Stacia said after she got her breath back.

"So what? I don't play music. I don't play anything but football." I crossed my arms and stuck my hands in my armpits, not wanting any more awful noise to come from me.

"Lucky you," she said. "I don't play anything *but* music. And apparently any instrument in my hands is now a lethal weapon." No blinking now; her eyes made her look like a rabbit caught under the foot of a fox—hunted and scared. "What's wrong with us?" she whispered.

"I don't know," I whispered back.

The waterworks started again. I just wanted to book it out of there. But I knew that screech would get me wherever I went. Plus, it didn't seem heroic to desert a damsel in distress, even if she was a famous Weird Band Girl.

I put my arm around her and handed her tissues. I hoped like heck she wasn't getting the wrong idea.

She sniffled, then honked a good one. "The thing is," she said, wiping her face, "everyone thinks I sound just fine. No one else hears it. And another thing—you and I don't even know each other. Why should we go insane together?"

"Mass hysteria" was what Pillsbury had called it. Stars over the goalpost. Flying out of tree houses and bunk beds. Screeching. Maybe someone was trying to tell Scott Schreiber and Stacia Caraviello something.

I just hoped it wasn't bad news.

10

PiLLSBURY STOOD iN FRONT OF SCiENCE class blowing hot air about his project. The kids sat stunned, as if a boredom bomb had exploded over them. Only Katelyn seemed to be listening as Pillsbury droned on. "Exponential growth in the *Rhus radicans toxicodendron* is postulated, based on historical data showing the mediated response to ultraviolet light . . ."

Our teacher, Mr. FitzPatrick, was asleep, his lumpy chin resting on a pile of books. His eyes were wide open but that didn't fool me. Every night, Pop did the same thing over his newspaper while Ma blabbered on about her beauty salon clients and their pathetic love lives.

Mr. FitzPatrick had a glob of a nose, a heavy chin, and sprouts of hair that poked from his bald head like the eyes of a rotting potato. His polo shirt clumped over his pillowy belly. Mr. Potato, we called him, because he looked like a scoop full of mush.

"Questions, anyone?" Mike asked.

DuCharme jerked to attention. "You done yet?"

"Let me rephrase that." Pillsbury glared. "Any intelligent questions?"

Katelyn raised her hand. "Mike, does this research have any practical application?" Katelyn Sands was one of the most popular girls in school but her taste in guys—specifically, Mike Pillsbury—was questionable.

"Unfortunately, no. I doubt anyone wants to promote the growth of *Rhus radicans*."

"Why not? What the heck is *roo*-whatever?" E.J. asked.

"Oh. I thought you all knew." Mike adjusted his glasses. "Poison ivy."

Poison ivy? And Pillsbury wondered why he didn't have more friends?

Mr. FitzPatrick triple-blinked his eyes, bringing his pupils into focus. "You covered it expertly, Mr. Pillsbury. A-plus work."

Pillsbury burst into a grin. How many times had I warned him? An atta-boy from a teacher combined with a big smile was an invitation for a whupping.

"Who is next?" Mr. FitzPatrick checked his seating chart. "Ah. Mr. Thorpe."

Silence.

Mr. FitzPatrick squinted at Mike as if he were hiding Thorpe under his chair. "Where is *Mis*ter Thorpe?"

DuCharme raised his hand but didn't wait to be called on. "Ask *Mis*ter Schreiber."

Pillsbury turned in his seat and peered through his glasses at me. "Where's Nick?"

I just shrugged.

DuCharme raised his hand again. At tomorrow's practice, I was going to kick that kid's butt from end to end, then punt him through the uprights. "*Mis*ter Thorpe got suspended for beating up *Mis*ter Schreiber."

FitzPatrick pushed his glasses up his lumpy forehead and stared at me. "Well, Mr. Schreiber, since you seemed to have survived your beating rather well—"

Nicole giggled, starting the class in an avalanche of laughter. I took it like a man takes a sacking: wait for it to be over, then plan revenge.

Mr. FitzPatrick signaled for silence. "Mr. Schreiber, please demonstrate your project, proving or disproving your thesis."

My butt was glued to my seat. Demonstrate what? Wasn't bringing in the nest enough? What was I supposed to say?

Pillsbury twisted around. "Your thesis," he hissed. "I told you to do a thesis statement and present

63

some supporting evidence. Remember?"

Somewhere, among the lights in the sky, the screeching in my head, and the strands of silver and gold, I vaguely remembered Pillsbury's yammering about a thesis.

"Mr. Schreiber? What's the matter? Did Mr. Thorpe damage your ability to speak?"

More laughter. I inched my way to the front. My classmates' projects were all around me, decorated with graphs, photos, typed pages. I had a nest in a box. And nothing to say. Why should I?

"Mr. Schreiber! Any time now!"

I set the nest on the table with the other projects. "I wanted to prove that just because you can't see something, it doesn't mean it doesn't exist. That you can find amazing things in unusual places, if you just look. In this case, I—"

I what? Ripped a tree apart while watching UFOs after a bear had chased me? "I dug this out from the middle of an injured tree. I was looking for a beehive or a bunch of bugs, but instead I found this nest. Proving that just because you can't see something, that doesn't mean it isn't there." I nodded at Mr. FitzPatrick, then headed back for my seat.

"Just a minute, Mr. Schreiber."

"Yeah?"

"Exactly what kind of nest is that?"

"Um. A bird's nest."

"What kind of bird?"

"The kind that builds its nest inside a tree."

"Why is that a bird's nest? Why not a squirrel's nest?"

"Squirrels don't make nests."

"Oh, really? How do you know that, Mr. Schreiber?"

"Because I've never seen a squirrel's—" My stomach plunged into my toes. I hadn't seen it coming.

FitzPatrick had sacked me.

"Hey, at least I didn't bring poison ivy to class." I glared at Pillsbury.

"You have not proven your thesis, Mr. Schreiber."

"Huh?"

"Huh? *Huh?* Allow me to simplify the statement—to match your intellect." More laughter. "This is F work. As in Failing. Flunking. Or, in your case, Futile."

"You're flunking me?" I yelled. "But Mr. FitzPatrick, it's an awesome nest."

"*Mis*ter Schreiber, my cat is an awesome cat. But you just can't put little Frisco on the table and call him a science project. You have been cognizant of the requirements of this project since September."

"I RISKED MY LIFE finding this nest!"

"The purpose of the science project is not to

prove what a hero you are. It is to propose and test a thesis. For example, Mr. Pillsbury tested the thesis of computer-mediated exposure to sunlight as it affects leaf development and photosynthesis. Even Mr. DuCharme—"

DuCharme? If Mr. FitzPatrick was using my buddy DuCharme as a good example, I was deader than the roadkill the cafeteria passed off as lunch meat.

"—even Mr. DuCharme had a thesis. Of course, it doesn't take a genius to postulate that if you smash a sunflower seed with a hammer, it's not going to germinate. But at least Mr. DuCharme took the time to propose, test, and report. He didn't just turn in a handful of chewed sunflower seeds and call them a science project. You give me no choice. Your grade is an F."

"I won't let you flunk me!" I yelled, my fists clenching.

"What are you going to do about it, Mr. Schreiber?" Mr. FitzPatrick straightened his bow tie and strutted over to me. "Mash me?"

11

HOW COULD PILLSBURY LET THIS happen to me? I had gotten home at five in the morning, exhausted. He should have known that I would forget to do the thesis paper.

I had one small hope that this stupid incident wouldn't interfere with the Super Bowl. Today was only Monday. Grades closed for the term on Wednesday. If Principal Goodrich didn't check them until after the holiday, I would be free and clear.

But as soon as I walked into the locker room that afternoon, I knew FitzPatrick had ratted me out. "Schreiber, get your lazy, no-good backside in here!" Coach Tremblay bellowed.

I slipped into his office, flinching under the sad stares of my teammates.

"How could you be so careless!" Coach roared.

His jowls shook with anger; his face turned fire-cracker red.

How could you *be so careless,* I wanted to roar back. *You should have assigned someone to watch my back. You kept me too busy winning games to keep track of all these stupid assignments.*

But I stayed silent, enduring fifteen minutes of Coach Tremblay's coffee breath in my face. Words like *irresponsible, thoughtless, careless, disgraceful, immature, ungrateful,* rat-a-tat-tatted me like a boxer pummeling his opponent.

I bucked up under the assault, praying that my teammates weren't listening at the door. Finally, Coach sputtered himself into exhaustion. "Get out of my face," he said, sighing. "I have no choice—you're off the team."

As I cleaned out my locker, my teammates gathered around me.

"No fair," Conner said, punching my arm.

"Sorry, Schreiber," DuCharme said. "If I knew FitzPatrick was gonna be such a SpudNik, I would have kept my mouth shut."

"Thith thtinkth," Fleming lisped. They still hadn't found his front teeth.

"You don't have to take this," Tenore said.

"What the heck can I do?" I whipped my locker shut. The whole row clanged with my frustration. "I need a Hail Mary play here or I'm done."

"What'th a Hail Mary?" Fleming asked.

"When you're backed against the end zone and out of time, you whip the ball as far as you can. All the way downfield, the full hundred yards if you have to. Then you pray someone catches it," DuCharme explained.

"Wait a minute. Let's think this out . . . you turned in the project, right?" Tenore asked. "Therefore, FitzPatrick's F is a subjective assessment."

"Huh?" I said. Tenore's big words made my brain fog thicker.

"It's not your fault if FitzPatrick didn't like it. He accepted Pillsbury's poison ivy, so why not your nest? We can claim discrimination, that FitzPatrick hates you 'cuz you're a jock and he's an egghead geek—"

"Better call him an academic," Keras said.

"Yeah, whatever. My dad's a lawyer. He could go to court tomorrow, get a stay of execution."

"Tenore, they don't kill you for flunking." Keras smirked.

"Not that kind of execution. He could ask for a hearing of the school board. They won't be able to schedule it until after Thanksgiving. So Schreiber will have to be allowed to play in the Super Bowl or SpudMan will be depriving him of his rights." Tenore puffed out his chest; brainy as well as brawny.

Hope glimmered in my mind, as sparkling as the strands in my nest. "Think it'll work?"

"Why not?" Tenore said. "My dad does this all the time, makes an honest living at it."

"Besides, it's not fair how FitzPuke treated you," Conner said.

"You tried, right?" Keras agreed. "Coach is only ripping because the SpudDud slammed Schreiber with all those lies. Otherwise, Tremblay would peel that potato and fry him good."

"Slander!" Tenore said. "We'll add that to the complaint. Discrimination and slander."

Just as they did on the field, the front line protected their quarterback.

"Do it, Schreiber."

"Come on, say yes."

"We need you to play."

"Besides, someone ought to teach SpitsPatrick a lesson," Clark growled.

"Someone ought to teach *Scott Schreiber* a lesson."

The guys went dead quiet. The only sound in the locker room was the overhead fan that sputtered and groaned but never got the sock stink out.

"What?" I said. "What did you say?"

Mike Pillsbury pushed through the crowd. "You heard me. Someone ought to teach you a lesson."

"Shut up, Dough Boy." Keras shoved Pillsbury.

Pillsbury sent him sprawling. Cripes, the kid was getting tough from hanging out with me.

Fleming lunged for Pillsbury but I yanked him off. "I don't need you defending me from this four-eyed, bony-butt turkey."

I got face-to-face with Pillsbury. My breath steamed his glasses. "What's your problem?"

"You," he said. "First you let Nick take the fall for you—"

"Thorpe admitted he attacked me."

"Nick is an idiot but he's not stupid. He would never hit you first. He wouldn't hit you last. And he's the one with the nose like a melon, not you."

"Yeah, well . . ." I wasn't about to add "liar" to Pillsbury's list of my faults. "Whatever happened, Thorpe and I worked it out, like friends."

"Friends? What do you know about friends? You treat your friends like something you scrape off the bottom of your sneaker."

"That's a load of bull," I shouted.

"Oh yeah? Did you tell the guys about last night? I told you exactly what to write in your report. But High-and-Mighty Schreiber is a hero. Just has to show up and get a free ride."

"I did the work," I protested.

"Some of it. Not all of it."

"You didn't help me like you promised." I sounded lame.

"I told you exactly what to do."

"Well, you heard the guys! It's FitzPotato's fault anyway."

"So instead of taking responsibility for your own carelessness, now you're gonna blame it all on Mr. FitzPatrick?"

"What, you want to see me fail, Pillsbury? Would that make you happy?"

"I want to see you take some responsibility, Scott."

"I don't need to get lectures from my friends," I snapped.

"I'm not your friend," Mike whispered. "Not anymore."

"Oh. Like that's the end of my life. I got news for you, Geekbury. I don't need friends like you. I'm Ashby's hero . . . or did you forget?"

The room was so quiet it was as if Mike and I were alone on the moon, so quiet that the whole team heard Mike Pillsbury when he said, "You are no hero, Schreiber. You are a coward."

I shot my fist at his face. But he ducked and I jammed my hand into a locker. As I cursed and moaned, Coach blew the whistle for practice.

"Tenore!" I called as I shook my fingers back to life. "Don't forget to ask your father."

"Actually, he's pretty busy these days," he said. "We'd better forget it."

"DuCharme?"

"Sorry, man. Stinko luck." As he caught up to Keras, I heard him say, "Hey, think Coach will give me a shot at quarterback?"

No one stopped to check my hand, no one brought me ice, no one gave Pillsbury the whipping he deserved. I was the only person left in the Schreiber universe. And I didn't much like my own company.

No one likes a coward.

12

BORN TO SOAR, i HAD NEVER BEEN

this low. The surface of the swamp rippled as hordes of Gargoyles stormed by, searching me out. Dim of mind, they wouldn't find me here, wouldn't even think to look. They would thrash the trees, looking for me to shelter in the Harna leaves. And when they didn't find me, they would erupt with fire and burn the forest to the ground.

The damp eased my burned feathers and the muck cushioned my broken bones. I submerged, only the tip of my beak out of the water to take in air. Overhead, wavering through the murky surface of the water, lights raced across the sky. Though the Gargoyles were passing, the real beasts had yet to step foot on this world. The Shards were glossy and bright, but their hearts were darker and emptier than any black hole.

I lay under the dank swamp, fearing their arrival. My mate was gone. My nest was gone. And, here, underwater, I couldn't even sing.

I had never been so alone.

"Scott Schreiber, wake up, you imbecile!"

"What? Where am I?" I tried to wipe mud out of my eyes. But it wasn't mud; my eyes were so heavy with sleep I couldn't force them open. When I finally did, the Weird Band Girl stared down at me.

"What're you doing here?" I mumbled.

"I live here," she said. "Good grief, what are the neighbors going to think? You snoring on my front step like a growling bear?"

I sat up and looked around: huge stone walls, broad lawns, big houses. I had biked to the far side of Ashby, among the mansions of the rich and some-times famous.

After I had left school, I didn't dare go home. How could I tell Ma I was off the football team? She'd yell and carry on, smother me in hugs and drown me in milk and cookies. Pillsbury's tree house was out. Whatever had made me think a genius-brained weirdo could be my friend? My real friends—if they were still my friends—were at foot-ball practice.

I had thought about hiding out at Thorpe's. Maybe I would let him beat me up for real so I wouldn't feel like such a slime. But even if I had both hands tied behind my back, I doubted Thorpe could put a dent in me. We'd just hang out and I wasn't in the mood for snorting and stupid jokes. So I went to see the one person in Ashby who was as miserable as I was—the Weird Band Girl, Stacia Caraviello.

I dropped my head into my hands. "Sorry."

"Scott, it's okay." Her voice, now soothing like cool water, made me realize how alone I was. Something inside me broke.

"Allergies," I said five minutes later, when I came out of her bathroom drying my eyes. Stacia Caraviello lived in a wonderland house like you see in those old black-and-white movies, where men strutted in tuxes and women lounged in slinky silk robes. Marble, glass, gold fixtures, polished wood—not the kind of place where you can toss a football.

"All the plants are dead in November," she said.

"It must be your cat," I said.

"No cats allowed in this house."

"Dog?"

"Oh please. Allow a dander-dropping canine in this house? I'm allowed rare tropical fish and a por-trait of snow wolves." She sat at the kitchen table with a plateful of fancy sandwiches, brownies, and cold milk. Table? It was more like a runway, longer than my entire kitchen. Two glasses were set out—

I guess that meant she was feeding me, too.

We munched in silence. Half of me was starved; the other half was on the verge of puking. I nibbled one brownie, ate a second, then gobbled the third. Nothing like sugar to give a guy a boost. "How's your music?" I asked.

"A nightmare," she said. "How's your football?"

"A nightmare," I said, and poured out the whole story: the fight that wasn't a fight, the bird's nest that might be a squirrel's nest, and the hero who was a creep.

I expected Stacia to order the butler to toss me out. Instead, she said, "Let's go see this nest."

"Why?" I asked.

"Just because."

"Just because why?" I asked again.

"Don't bug me about this. I usually don't do things *just because*," she said. "But something is telling me to see the nest."

She fiddled her fingers on the table, then looked up at me. "It's like when I'm performing and I know a change in the tempo or tone is coming. I *feel* it even before the conductor signals it. *Just because*." She sighed. "You probably think I'm nuts."

"Well, you probably are." I sighed back. "But if you're nuts, I'm nuts too. So let's go."

"There it is," Stacia gasped as we turned from her road onto Main Street. I didn't even have to ask what "it" was; the steady buzz in my head intensified into scratching, then scraping, then that awful screech.

The closer we got to the school, the louder the screeching became. We stuffed our ears with our fingers, held our breath, recited multiplication tables. Nothing stopped the assault.

"You're not even playing music," I said, confused.

"Wait, I have an idea. Don't say anything."

I shut up. For a moment, the screech died out. Then it roared back. "What the heck!" I yelped.

"It's gotten beyond the music," Stacia gasped, her eyes blinking up a storm. "Now it happens when we talk—notice how loud it is now. Shhh. Hear it? Even when we think too hard."

"I've never been accused of thinking too hard," I said. We laughed and the screech almost shattered us. All around us, people drove cars, walked dogs, raked the last of the autumn leaves. No one else heard it.

"We're only a block away," she said. "Let's try to keep our minds blank and just get to that nest."

I let my mind go gray, the way it used to be before Mike Pillsbury filled it with weirdness and excitement. The screech lessened. Stacia stared straight ahead. It would be harder for her—she was an artist. Even that thought sent shock waves through me.

Gray. Neutral. Nothing.

Stacia stumbled against me. At the back door of the school, the screech was murderous. I took her hand. "A few more steps," I whispered. "Stay with me."

Gray, step. Nothing, step. *What if someone sees me holding the hand of a Weird Band Girl?* Screech, breathe, step. *Anyone says anything, I'll give 'em a knuckle sandwich.*

Inside the school, the screech blasted us with hurricane force. Harry, the night custodian, glanced up from his mop, gave us a wave, and got back to washing floors, clueless about the screech that was tearing us up.

I guided Stacia to FitzPatrick's classroom. What if the Potato had destroyed my nest? After all, to him it was a big fat F. But I snapped on the lights and there it sat on the table. Screaming at us.

Stacia's long fingers moved with a delicate grace as she touched the strands. "They're scared."

"Who?" I gasped, trying not to collapse as the screech plagued my brain like bolts of lightning.

The ships landed like a plague of lightning— fast, deadly, pervasive. The Shard rang chaos on the friendly Centaurs. They huddled under brush or shivered in caves as the sharp ones sparked through their land, searching for me.

I wanted to sing my Centaur friends a song of

79

courage and comfort but I didn't dare rise from the mire. The cool shadows were my only hope of escape—if my fear didn't ripple the water and alert the seekers to my hiding place.

I was so scared.

I was on my knees, dying under the screech.

"It's okay," Stacia said. "They're not trying to hurt us, they're just scared."

"Who?" I gasped again.

"Them," she said. Then she slipped her hand into the nest, twisting her fingers and maneuvering her wrist so she could fit. The screech stopped.

The silence was pure mercy.

"It's okay now," she said, but not to me. Stacia pulled out something small and round, like a Ping-Pong ball but a deep purple. As she put it in my hand, it grew warm and I dimly realized it wasn't a ball at all.

It was an egg. And it needed holding. I put it to my face and the music began.

Stacia grinned at me. "You hear it, don't you? Listen carefully—they're tiny notes. Like fairy bells or hummingbird whispers." She brought out two more eggs. The music grew louder and happily confused, like little kids laughing in a sprinkler or puppies yipping as they tumble.

Stacia hummed a soothing tune. "Brahm's Lullaby," she whispered. I tried to sing along but it came out as a yodel, so I put my cheek next to hers so my egg could share in her music.

And that's really the meaning of it all, that we make the music that brings us together. Stars and light and love and creation, soaring to the great certainty that binds us all in perfect pitch . . .

And then, in the middle of this brain-injured daydream, I knew. "They need us to take care of them," I whispered. "Until we get them back to their parents."

"What are their parents?" Stacia whispered, then continued humming. "Some rare birds?"

"It's not what. It's who."

"Who? You talk like they're human," she said.

"Not human," I said. "But people just the same."

"Are you insane?" she whispered. The eggs chirped and Stacia resumed her quiet singing.

"Nope," I said. "Just a little weird."

13

YESTERDAY i HAD WALKED iNTo SCHooL on air, feeling ten feet tall. I was the Mighty Schreiber, king of a world where kids cheered, teachers congratulated, and girls swooned.

Today everyone in town knew that Scott Schreiber had flunked out of the Super Bowl. Ma had blubbered all last night. Pop hid behind the newspaper, sitting in his chair until midnight and never once turning a page. This morning on the bus, the kids talked and laughed and ignored me. What can you say to a hero who's blown it big time?

But low as I was, a small part of me was flying. I had a secret—the eggs nestled at Stacia's house. Take away football, take away my friends, but no one was taking those eggs from us. The Weird Band Girl and I were our own team, guardians of those

82

eggs until we could find their rightful parents.

I had wanted to take the whole nest home but Stacia had said no. "They were screeching to get out of the nest," she reasoned. "We can't put them back in."

The screech—our eggs' cry for help—was gone. Last night, Stacia was like a kid at Christmas, grabbing every instrument she owned to serenade the eggs. I listened and tapped my foot and let out an occasional yodel. For the first time in my life, I envied someone else's talent.

Stacia made the music and the music made everything right.

So, as I walked into science class, where yesterday I had been humiliated, embarrassed, and flunked, it wasn't the total end of the world.

Mr. FitzPatrick was aflutter, like a moth bumping at a lightbulb. "Mr. Schreiber, I've been waiting for you. There's someone here to meet you."

A huge man towered over the Potato. "My name is John Cutter." His suit jacket strained over his muscular shoulders. As we shook hands, mine disappeared in his giant paw. His hand was strong and ice cold. His hair looked steel gray, but when he turned his head, each separate strand seemed to reflect overhead lights like thousands of tiny mirrors. But his eyes were dark, so dark that they seemed to suck in all the light.

"Um . . . hi," I muttered. A guy that big and that well put together had to be a football scout. Did this Cutter fellow know I was now ineligible?

"That's quite a nest you've got there," John Cutter said.

"You're not here about football?"

"No, I'm an environmental scientist." He handed me a business card.

JOHN CUTTER

Special Agent

ENVIRONMENTAL PRESERVATION AGENCY

A scientist who looked like a football player! Maybe there was hope for Pillsbury yet.

"I found the nest in Willard Forest. But I didn't have a chance"—I glared at the Potato—"to identify it."

"That won't be necessary," Cutter said.

"Why not?"

"Because I'll be taking possession of it."

That fumble urge switched on inside me, and I almost stuffed the nest under my arm and dashed out of there. But with those broad shoulders and monster

84

hands, John Cutter could take me down in a flash.

"Excuse me, sir. But it's my nest," I said as politely as I knew how.

"Nevertheless, I am taking it," Cutter said.

FitzPatrick grinned like a hyena. "Your nest has been identified as belonging to a rare avian species. If you allow Mr. Cutter to take it to its proper setting you will be doing a great service. And to reward you, I will change your grade to a C."

"You mean, I won't be flunked?"

"No, you won't. You apparently have discovered an ecological treasure. And that discovery deserves recognition."

My world flipped upright. I could play in the Super Bowl! Yesterday would be just a bad dream. Except yesterday wasn't all a bad dream—what about the eggs? Football. The Super Bowl. Eggs. Music. The Weird Band Girl—holding her hand, listening to her sing. I was dizzy, trying to sort all out. "I need to think about it."

John Cutter got in my face. "You really don't have a choice, young Schreiber. What the agency wants, the agency gets."

I glanced at my classmates. DuCharme was waving like a fool, urging me to say yes. Monroe gave me a thumbs-up. Katelyn smiled.

Pillsbury wouldn't even look at me.

"Give him the stupid nest," DuCharme hissed.

85

"Yeah," E.J. added. "It's dirty and smelly. Get it out of here."

"I just don't know . . ." I muttered. *Pillsbury, give me a sign! Tell me what to do!* But Mike's eyes stayed glued to his book.

FitzPatrick guided me to a corner for a whispered conference. "Mr. Schreiber, though I won't let football interfere with academics, I took a lot of flack for flunking you. It appears that this nest is a way out of our dilemma. So why don't you just give it to the man and get on with your life? And let me get on with mine."

What harm could it do? Stacia had the eggs and now that they were out of the nest, they had stopped shrieking. What good was the nest anyway? It felt cold, empty. No longer beautiful. Was that because Stacia had taken the eggs out? Or was it because I was about to trade my nest for my football career? Football or eggs? Hero or weirdo?

What weirdo wouldn't choose to be normal, given the chance?

I handed the nest to Special Agent Cutter. His dazzling smile made the hairs on the back of my neck rise.

What had I done?

At practice, the guys were all over me, glad to have me back on the team. Even DuCharme punched me silly. "Coach put me at QB and I got clobbered," he moaned.

I grabbed Pillsbury on the way out to the practice field. "See," I gloated. "I did something scientifically important."

"Grow up," he said. "It was all a put-on."

"You heard the guy. That nest is rare. Special." And not alien, I thought, not if the United States government knew about it.

"How did some big shot from Washington hear about a middle school science project? Someone cooked up this Cutter guy to get you back in the game," Pillsbury said.

"That's nuts. Look at his card." I dashed back to my locker and dragged it out of my bag.

JOHN CUTTER
Special Agent
ENVIRONMENTAL PRESERVATION AGENCY

"I knew it!" Pillsbury sneered. "The guy is one fat fake."

"You don't know everything!"

"I know this: The EPA is the Environmental

Protection Agency, not *Preservation* Agency. It's all a ruse," Pillsbury said, "just to get you eligible for the Super Bowl. How many people are you going to let lie for you, Scott?"

"What's it to you?" I snarled. Pillsbury's constant lectures made me want to lecture him back—with my fists.

"What's it to me? I thought—after the Jong and all—that you were the real thing," Mike said. "But you're just all flash and no fire."

"And you're all crap," I said. I pulled on my helmet and ran onto the field, ready to kill, kill, kill. Maybe Coach would put Pillsbury on the front line against me.

Then I would show him fire.

14

NO ONE COULD LAY A HAND ON ME AT
practice. Running, passing, commanding the troops—
the Mighty Schreiber was unstoppable. With all the
cheering and yelling and charging, I forgot about
the fairy bells and hummingbird whispers until I
biked home.

The eggs! I had promised Stacia to come see
them after school. And now it was supper time. Ma
had promised to make pork stew and pumpernickel
bread to celebrate my return to football. "I just hope
it isn't your last meal," she said with a sigh when I
called her with the news. "Football is so dangerous."

Pop wouldn't say a word, but he would turn the
pages of his newspaper and laugh at the comics. His
short laugh goes a long way. I was starved and tired
and dying to be home. And what did I need with the

eggs anyway? Funny little bird eggs that would probably just rot and smell in a few days.

What else could they be but bird eggs?

. . . wondering if my children would ever take flight. I would never lift my wings again but it wouldn't matter, not if the past, future, and forever now of our music was safe. But where are my eggs?

Augh! I smacked my forehead, trying to shake out all the crazy thoughts. First the flying, then the screeching, then these crazy stories in my head. My head was like a radio that had been set to some sort of opera station and I didn't understand a word of what was bouncing through my airwaves.

Too much Mike Pillsbury. Sure, we had seen real aliens—fought bad aliens and saved good aliens last month. But they were never, *ever* coming back. We had been told clearly and sternly by the galactic powers—never again.

It was time to put all this alien stuff behind me. That flying business had been just a bad dream, or maybe a rattled brain from too many tackles. Despite what Pillsbury said, I had to believe the nest was just a bird's nest, like John Cutter said it was. And thanks to John Cutter, it was time to get on with the business of winning the Super Bowl.

I pedaled harder. X's and O's and spirit songs crowded my head, along with visions of soaring footballs and crashing bodies. This is what I was born for, what I lived for. So why did those fairy bells and hummingbird whispers keep leaking into my brain?

I stopped two blocks from my house and called home. "I'll keep your supper warm, Scottie!" Ma shouted. The woman didn't even need phone lines to get her point across.

As I skidded to a stop at the bottom of Stacia's driveway, a car pulled alongside me. Sleek and low, the vehicle sparkled like diamonds. *Figures*, I thought. *Everyone in this neighborhood is stinking rich.*

John Cutter stepped out of the passenger side. "I've been looking for you, young Schreiber."

I fumbled with the gate. Through the iron fence, the lights in Stacia's house shone, warm and inviting. Music wafted across the lawn. The latch was stuck. "Yeah, well, sorry, can't stop to talk. I'm busy."

"So am I," Cutter said. He grabbed me around the neck.

The Shard sparkled like aluminum foil. His eyes were crystal tunnels, flashing with silver that swirled deeper and deeper, disappearing into deep sockets. His fingers were long and smooth, tipped with claws as sharp as knife blades.

His hands clutched my throat.

John Cutter's hands clutched my throat.

Mike's story wasn't a story at all—it was real, all

the time. REAL! I begged my feet to keep still because I knew—from my dreams or my injured brain, or from someone's distant warning—I knew not to move. John Cutter, Special Agent or Shard, could slice off my head with the flick of a finger.

"What do you want?" I whispered. "I gave you the nest."

"I want what was inside the nest."

"There was nothing inside the nest." Another lie but one even Pillsbury would forgive me.

His fingers tightened, pinching my skin. My throat was only a millimeter away from being sliced. "The eggs," he said. "Give me the eggs."

I will die before I let these beasts get our children. Fly away now! Fly high and long and I will stand firm here and fight.

The cries rattled inside my aching head. *I believe, I believe. Now help me to fly!* I shouted back in my mind. But my feet stayed on the ground, held in place by Cutter's dagger hands. So fight it was. But how? *What do I do?* I begged of the music of the stars. *What do I do?*

"I'm losing patience, young Schreiber." Cutter squeezed tighter. Something trickled under my ear, warm and thick. Not sweat, not tears. Blood.

I tensed my right foot, ready to raise my knee into his groin. "I don't know what you're talking about," I lied again.

"Well, then. That makes you completely disposable, doesn't it?"

I kicked and—*BAM!*—Cutter went down. But he was up in a flash, his dagger hands clicking furiously at me. I turned to run but he caught me easily. "Disposable." He laughed, strangling me.

I went down, drowning in a deep red haze that exploded into a million shining stars.

Music rang at me from all directions. I was a liar and a coward but I still made it through the Pearly Gates! Touchdown!

"Scottie!" Ma roared. I forced open my eyes. Heaven was a big bedroom with heavy blue drapes, a roaring fireplace, and a four-poster bed.

"Where am I?" I moaned. My neck was covered with bandages. "Am I dead?"

Dr. Faulkenham stepped to the bed. "You're fine, Scott."

"My baby!" Ma cried, and swept me into her arms.

"The neck, Marge!" my father said in a low voice.

"What happened?" I moaned, untangling myself from my mother's iron grip.

A very thin woman dressed in a blue suit and wearing gold earrings leaned over the bed. "I'm Stacia's mother, Scott. Sorry to make your acquaintance under such distressing circumstances," she said. "You rode your bike into our

93

iron fence. I'm afraid you got cut up a bit."

"You took a few stitches here and there. But you're okay," Dr. Faulkenham said.

"Okay? My boy got impaled on a steel fence and you think he's okay?" Mom roared.

"I hardly think he was impaled," Mrs. Caraviello said in a voice that could freeze hot pepper. "He stumbled and needed a few stitches."

Ma got in her face. "A few stitches? How'd you like me to show you a few stitches, huh, lady?"

I pulled the covers over my head. If Ma put her famous headlock on Mrs. Caraviello, I'd never be able to show my face again!

Dr. Faulkenham stepped between the two mothers. "You are fine, Scott. However, we might want to get your head checked again—"

I bolted up in the bed. "No!"

"Yes," my father said.

"Forget football!" my mother barked. "Just get your head better."

It wasn't football I was worried about.

Mrs. Caraviello insisted I spend the night in their guest room. My mother almost burst a blood vessel trying to get me to come home but I said I just wanted to sleep. As Pop dragged her out of the room, she shouted instructions for my care and feeding. Dr. Faulkenham promised to stop by in the morning—if I was as good as I claimed, she would let me go to school.

I wanted everyone gone so I could talk to Stacia. As my parents' old Dodge putt-putted down the winding driveway, Stacia came in. She had a tray with sandwiches, milk, fruit, cookies, and a small basket. Our eggs, shining and strong, sat on a velvet cloth.

"Are they okay?" I said, touching one lightly.

"Fine." Her face was as white as the cold glass of milk on my tray. "It wasn't the fence that cut you up."

I held an egg to my face. Their music was a tiny hum; they must be sleeping. "I know. What happened?"

"I was playing my guitar, singing to the eggs. Then I realized my parents had locked the gate and you wouldn't be able to get in. When I ran down to unlock it, I saw that man strangling you. Blood was gushing everywhere!" She shuddered. "You were going limp. I didn't even think, I just bashed the man over the head with my guitar. And then . . ."

Her face crumpled. I took her hand. It was soft. "Then what?" I said.

"He shattered into a million pieces and just blew away on the wind." She clenched my hand so hard my knuckles cracked. "What did I do, Scott? Did I kill a man?"

"Not a man," I said. And I told her what we had

been forbidden to tell any Earthling: how a few weeks ago Mike Pillsbury called the aliens, and how together we had rescued the Hanzels and Mike's neighbor, little Jay, from the Jong. It had all been weird, like a crazy dream, but it had all been real. Now the flying, the screeching, the eggs, and the Shards—the most dangerous dudes in the known universe—were turning out to be real, too.

"You're delusional," Stacia cried.

"You shattered a guy into a million pieces and you're saying I'm nuts?" I sighed, exhausted.

"No," Stacia whispered. "I guess you're not nuts." She fingered the eggs. A lovely sound, like no sound on Earth, fluttered from the shells. "We need some help. I'd better tell my parents."

"We can't tell anyone. Anyone!" I said. "Earth has protected status. If knowledge of any aliens becomes widespread, then we lose that status."

"So what?"

"We aren't ready for galactic membership," I explained. "Earth could be neutralized."

"Neutralized?" she cried. "What's that?"

"You don't want to know."

"We can't tell the FBI or the army or our parents that evil aliens are loose on our planet?" she moaned. "So who can we tell?"

The cuts on my neck hurt but I grinned anyway. "Mike Pillsbury. He'll know what to do."

15

WHEN i PHONED HiM AT MiDNiGHT,
Mike Pillsbury had two words for me: "Stuff it!"

"You gotta listen to me!" I begged. "They're back. Well, they're not back. These are new ones, like the Shards in your story!" After I told him about the screeching and Stacia and the eggs and John Cutter, Pillsbury had two more words for me.

"You're disgusting." He slammed down the phone.

I dialed back. "Why did you say I was disgusting?"

"You got your life as a big football hero. What do you want my life for?"

"What are you talking about, you ignorant moron?"

"You're the ignorant one, Scott. Making up lies

about aliens to make yourself look important. And you can't even come up with your own aliens—you have to steal mine."

"They're not lies! I have proof. Stitches!"

"A fence that you were too stupid to ride around. That's what your mother said when she called asking me to get your homework."

"My ma wouldn't call me stupid."

"No, I drew that conclusion myself," Mike sneered.

"You gotta listen! The Shards have the nest and now they want the eggs."

"Okay. Let's say these Shards are real and not just you ripping off my stories . . ."

"They are real!" I shouted.

"So then, how much can that nest mean to you if you gave it up for a chance to play lousy football?"

"Football's not lousy! Besides, it wasn't like that. Why won't you believe me?" I begged.

"Here's why I won't believe you, Scott. If there were aliens in trouble, they wouldn't come to you. They would come to me. And they have not come to me."

"But—" I protested.

"Therefore, they do not exist." Pillsbury slammed the phone down.

I didn't bother calling back.

* * *

The next morning, Dr. Faulkenham approved me for school and football practice. "But no contact today," she said. "We don't want those stitches opening."

The Caraviellos' cook served a breakfast of Belgian waffles with imported strawberries and Vermont maple syrup. Ma called three times to make sure I had enough to eat. Mr. Caraviello drove us to school in a car bigger than my dad's garage.

"Your friend won't help us? What are we going to do?" Stacia asked when we were finally alone.

"Call for help," I said. "That's how Pillsbury did it." But all my fiddling in shop class that afternoon couldn't produce an intergalactic SOS. I had almost given up when I saw a TV truck setting up on the football field for Friday's Super Bowl. A truck with huge satellite dishes on its roof.

"Hey, want an interview?" I asked the technician.

"Who are you?" he growled, trying to piece a cable together.

"Ashby's quarterback. Scott—"

"The Mighty Schreiber!" The guy glanced up at me, his eyes bright. "Let me get the boss."

Two minutes later I was on camera. A slick woman peppered me with questions about our offensive strategy, our special teams, our training routines. Finally, she gave me something I could work with: "I understand you've had some injuries this week. A bump on the head. Some stitches?"

"Oh yeah, it's been a rough week." I stared straight into the camera. "I had some unexpected visitors. From a place called Pav—" What planet had Pillsbury mentioned in his Chronicle? "Pavement!"

"That's nice, Scott. Now about your draw play—"

"These people from Pavement were real cut-ups. As sharp as glass."

"That's nice. But back to football—"

I took the microphone out of her hand. "They've been a real nuisance and won't go away. I'm hoping my friends from Sirius will come."

"Serious? Where's that, Kansas?" she asked with a fake smile. She was ready to throttle me.

"A little farther out. But I really need them to make the game, even though it's a long trip."

She motioned for me to return the microphone. I smiled and stared into the camera. "We can't survive unless they're here to support us."

The lady made the cut motion to her cameraman. He reached for the off switch on his videocam but I grabbed his hand and crunched his knuckles.

"I'm counting on them, especially my cousin Barnabus." *Come on, Barnabus, hear me,* I prayed. Barnabus had been the first and best alien to respond when Pillsbury called for help.

I continued my pitch. "We have some cheers we want them to help us with. Singing cheers I learned from my friend Lyra. But I need Barnabus's help—"

The sports lady pulled the plug. "You stupid kid," she snapped. "Anyone ever tell you that you're just a little weird?"

A little weird? I hoped I was big enough weird to get the message out there.

Way out there.

My teammates caught the show on the television in Coach's office. Crisostamo and LeSieur thought I was funny enough to be in movies. Fleming wanted to get interviewed until Shattuck reminded him that he was still missing his front teeth.

Pillsbury split a gut. "Are you nuts! It's forbidden!" Pillsbury yelled. "You'll get yourself fried. Maybe get all of us fried for unauthorized transmission."

"All I did was give an interview. Football heroes do that sort of thing." I turned on the shower and soaped up.

"You tried to call for help!" Pillsbury muttered, shampoo running down his face.

"I did call for help," I reminded him. "But you refused."

"You better hope no one answers. It could be the

end of you. The end of all of us. Some hero, putting us all in danger of getting neutralized."

I turned off the water and threw a towel around my waist. As I trotted to my locker, Pillsbury yammered at my back. "And it's *Pavo*, not Pavement, you idiot!"

I hoped like heck someone from somewhere would answer, whether it be Sirius or Sewer. Stacia and I needed help. John Cutter—or some creature who looked just like him—had been at football practice, watching from the sidelines.

We needed a wind strong enough to blow him away for good.

16

ASHBY CENTER BUZZED WITH EXCITE-
ment. People jammed the stores, buying cranberry
sauce, turnips, and pumpkin pies to go with tomorrow's turkey and stuffing.

Ma had asked me to pick up her bird on my way
home from practice. "You're such a strong boy,
Scottie," she said. "And Joe the butcher loves to see
you in his store." While Joe was out back wrapping
Ma's gobbler, I strolled the aisles, listening for an
answer to my call.

"Psst," I whispered to the lobster tank. "Anyone
in there?" The lobsters bubbled and tumbled, ignoring me. I dug through boxes of cookies and snack
cakes—that's where I would hide if I were an alien.

I ducked out to the back alley and checked Joe's
Dumpster. "Anyone there?" I gasped, holding my

nose. *Yowl!* An alley cat leaped at me, clutching a fish carcass in his mouth. "Kitty?" I called hopefully as it dashed into the darkness.

Inside, Joe finally had Ma's turkey ready. "It was a lively bird," he boasted, wiping his hands on his stained apron. My gut twisted. What if the turkey had been my alien? No, it couldn't be. Aliens were smart—they wouldn't send turkeys here the night before Thanksgiving.

I cycled home, singing a stupid song. *Is anyone here to help me? I'm all alone, my eggs in one basket, my butt in another. Who will come from far away*—"AND I MEAN FAR AWAY!" I shouted—*and help me?*

A dog howled. "Barnabus?" I called.

"Shut up that infernal singing!" a voice shrieked. "You're making my dog nuts!"

Ma greeted me at the back door, hugging my neck so hard I thought the stitches would burst. "Do your old lady a favor. Mallory Hardy is here for a last-minute perm. Wash out the turkey and put it in the fridge for me." She kissed me, smelling like hair spray, and hustled back to the shop in our basement.

I plopped the turkey into the sink. Its wings flopped apart and its midsection gaped open. That was it! The perfect hiding place so John Cutter wouldn't suspect other aliens were in town.

I flipped the turkey on its head—where the head used to be—and poked inside. "You can come out now," I whispered. "Ma's downstairs."

Nothing.

"It's okay," I said. "It's me, the Mighty Schreiber. You saw me on TV. I'm the one who called for you. Come on out."

Nothing.

I stuck my hand in. Cold and slippery, just like an alien should feel. I yanked out a fistful of dark red mush. "Move it!" I roared. "I could use a little help here."

"Thanks, sweetie," Ma yelled, and grabbed the mush away. "I came back upstairs to get this going." Before I could stop her, she dropped the blob into a pot of boiling water.

"Ma, what're you doing?"

"Cooking the guts," she hollered. "Your father loves giblet gravy with his turkey."

Forget the turkey. My goose was cooked and it wasn't even Thanksgiving yet.

I wandered into the family room to congratulate my father on his giblets. A huge, furry creature sat in my father's recliner reading the newspaper and smoking a cigar.

"Bear!" I gasped, and bolted out. I slammed the door hard and leaned against it, trying not to pee

105

my pants. Where was my father? Had that bear finally gotten his Schreiber special?

My poor pop. Why should he suffer because I was a magnet for creeps and creatures? I sucked it up and went back in. The bear put down the paper. "You done freaking out, buster?"

I grabbed a lamp and raised it over my head. "Where's my father?"

"Out buying dog food." The bear laughed. "He likes me, said he'd get the expensive stuff."

"Dog food?" I sputtered. "But you're a—" I stepped closer, keeping the lamp ready. Though he was certainly big enough, the beast was not a bear. He had a square face, round paws, long black fur, and a mighty tail. "You're a dog," I whispered.

"And you're as lamebrained as Barnabus said you were," he growled. He threw back his huge head and a little box peeked out from under his neck. Like the aliens we had met last month, this guy wore the translator collar that made sense out of anyone's words.

"I'm a Sirian. Ditka is my name; enforcement is my game."

"You actually came!"

Ditka sniffed me up and down, his snout flaring. "I've been here for days, running an operation. Which you stuck your stinky puss in the middle of, you furless fool! I've been too busy tracking down the

106

nest to thank you properly for screwing everything up." He bared his teeth—unlike Barnabus, who had polite poodle teeth, this guy had huge chompers.

Aimed at my face.

"Hey, I thought you Sirians were peacekeepers," I said, backing into the wall.

Ditka rose to his hind legs, towering over me. "I'm on the muscle side of the organization. When everything else fails, they send me in."

"I'm on your side," I said. "I'm trying to take care of the eggs."

"The eggs?" Ditka howled. "Kibbles and Bits!"

Ditka leaped for me and my life flashed before my eyes—a hundred touchdowns, a thousand cheers, a million dreams. As I crashed to the floor under Ditka's paws, the regrets piled up, all the things I had never done, would never get to do. Play in the NFL. Drive a big truck. Have a bunch of girl-friends. Sing instead of yodel. Make peace with Pillsbury. Tell my ma to shut up and listen, for once. Hug my dad instead of shake hands all the time.

Listen to more music.

Ditka opened his mouth, his sharp teeth an inch from my face. I sucked in what I thought was my last gasp, cursing his nasty cigar breath.

Then he licked my face, up one side and down the other! "What a good boy, finding the eggs!" he slobbered. "You can help me!"

I pushed him off me. Slurp dripped down my cheeks. "I'm the one who needs help. John Cutter— I think he's a Shard—tried to kill me. He has the nest and he wants the eggs."

Ditka hunched his back. "The Shards are here already? Sticks and stones!" he cursed. "I'm too late. I failed and they're going to assign me to that nasty Itchall planet where the fleas and ticks run wild."

"Chill out!" I said. "I'll do anything. Just tell me what."

"Okay, let me think about this. We got the eggs— so we need to get the mother," he panted. "The Lyra."

"Where is she?"

"I don't know," he said, his eyes drooping. "Even though I was sent to help her, she isn't talking to me." His ears perked up. "But she must be talking to you, if you've got the eggs."

"No," I said. "She's not. But I think I know some-one she might talk to."

17

STACIA BLINKED INTO OVERDRIVE. "A bear that talks!" she gasped.

"A dog that talks," I corrected.

"A Sirian that talks," Ditka growled. "And bites when provoked. So don't bug me!"

"Scott, I can't do this! I'm not allowed out in the middle of the night. And certainly not with a football player and a talking"—Ditka bared his fangs and Stacia sweetened her tone—"a talking visitor."

"You have to," I begged. "We need to find the eggs' mother."

"Don't you lecture me, Scott Schreiber. You traded the nest for a chance to play football!"

"I didn't mean to!" I cried. "I didn't know better."

"Well, I do. I'm going to be their mother," she huffed, falling into a lawn chair. We had come out to her backyard to talk. Dogs—or creatures resembling dogs—were not allowed in her house. "I'm taking care of them. Protecting them."

Ditka flattened his ears. "Cats and rats! Can you defend them against that, Earth girl?" He pointed his snout at the sky. The cold night seemed endless.

"I don't see anything," she said.

My knees went spaghetti-floppy. "I do. Look, Stacia. Look carefully."

Stacia squinted. "Oh, my." A fleet of spaceships hovered over us, like see-through jellyfishes swimming our sky, waiting to sting.

"Why isn't the air force chasing them, shooting them down?" I asked.

"Your sensing devices are primitive," Ditka snorted. "The only people who can see a Shard ship are people who are *sensitive* to such things."

"What things?" Stacia asked.

"The mysterious, wonderful, and terrible things of the universe that are beyond most people's imagination," he said. "Apparently, Barnabus's friend Mike Pillsbury has always been a sensitive. Scott was sensitized through Mike, and you, Stacia, well, you seem to be an exceptional listener. Even though Earth is off-limits, the rest of the universe leaks through to people like you. Like now—do you hear what those ships are saying?"

Stacia covered her ears. "I don't want to know."

"We have to know," I snapped. "What are they saying?"

"Surrender the eggs!" Ditka snarled.

"Never!" Stacia and I said together.

"What do we do?" she cried.

"If we find the mother, I can get her off this planet and the Shards will leave." Ditka said. "We need you to listen for her, Caraviello."

"Me? Why me?"

"Because you know *how* to listen," I said. "You know music."

"I know Earth music," Stacia moaned. "Stravinsky, Gershwin, Vivaldi. I don't know outer space music."

"Come on, Stacia. You can do it," I said.

"I'm not even supposed to be outside this late at night!"

"And eggs aren't supposed to be without their mothers," I said.

"Help me, then." Stacia closed her eyes and reached out her hand. Her fingers shook like a dry leaf battered by the wind. "Please."

Did I want to hold the hand of a Weird Band Girl again? Absolutely not. But Stacia Caraviello's hand, with her soft skin and strong fingers—yes, I thought, maybe I could hold her hand.

It was for the good of the universe, after all.

Stacia concentrated while I watched the night.

Overhead, the ships twinkled like lights on a Christmas tree. How awesome the Shards could be—if they weren't the nastiest dudes this side of the Milky Way. Ditka prowled the yard, scratching and growling. "Blowhards and Shards! Just let them try something."

Stacia dug her fingernails into my palm. Her hand was slick with sweat even though it was chilly outside. "It's okay," I promised, with no clue how it could be okay.

Then Stacia opened her eyes and smiled. "It is okay. I know where she is."

Stacia had never ridden a bike in her life. "I'm not allowed," she explained. "Because of the risk to my hands." So we drove her father's golf cart through backyards and ball fields, all the way to Willard Forest.

"This is living!" Ditka howled as the cold wind blew the fur back from his face. His eyes were huge and wild. His tongue flapped, drinking in the crisp autumn air.

"Hey, Dead Bolt," I sneered. "You ride in space-ships, remember? They go a little faster than this hunk of junk."

"We're a nonprofit agency," he whimpered. "We never get to go first-class."

"This way!" Stacia yelled. I banked a hard right,

plowing through a clump of brush. The golf cart took the bumps and holes like a tank. "It's fortified," Stacia explained. "Had to be—my dad is the world's worst golfer, spends a lot of time in the rough."

We slogged through the forest, far off the main path. The cart had headlights but the bouncing shadows were scarier than the dark wall of night. "This is nowhere near where I found the nest. We didn't get this deep into the woods," I said. I was panting, trying to keep the cart upright as it went over rocks and fallen trees. "Are you sure you know where you're going?"

"My job is to figure out where we're going. Yours is to get us there. So shut up and let me listen."

Stacia sat perfectly calm, listening and humming as we bounced deeper into the woods. Finally, she said, "Stop."

I jammed on the brakes and thanked the stars above that we were still alive.

"Here," she said. "Here" was the darkest part of Willard Forest, trees crowding overhead and prickers grabbing us from every side. The moon still slept. The stars twinkled, small but unfriendly, quadrillions of miles away. The only light was the bubble-glimmer of the Shard ships—hanging overhead like a pack of hungry vultures.

"Where?" I asked.

"Up there." "Up there" was an ancient pine tree that stretched straight into the black night.

"You're in charge of this operation," I snapped at Ditka. "Now what?"

"You go up and get her," he said.

"Me? You're the enforcer!"

"Dogs don't climb trees, Scott," Stacia said.

"He's a Sirian!" I yelped. "He has no excuse for not going up!"

"Sirians don't climb trees," he growled. "That's what you monkey-pawed Earthlings are for."

"Hey, you got the tail, Bow Wow."

"But you've got the ape fingers, Bald Face."

"You want a one-way trip to the dog pound?" I yelled.

"You want a one-way trip to the Shard heap?" Ditka snarled back.

Stacia took my hand. I tried to yank it away but she was too strong. "Scott, please. She says to send her the hero. That's you."

The hero.

The Mighty Schreiber.

Ashby's finest.

I didn't want to climb a tree higher than my imagination. I didn't want Shards disposing of me. I didn't want Ditka chewing on my leg. I didn't want to be a hero. I just wanted to play football and pretend I was a hero.

But I didn't want our eggs to go without their mother.

"I'll do it," I said. "But I don't have a clue how."

We couldn't call the fire department, the rescue squad, or the air force. We had no ladder, no rope, no climbing tools. How could I climb a tree that went twenty feet up before branches sprouted? No way could I shinny—the trunk was too broad to wrap my arms around. And what if the tree were rotten, like the one I found the nest in?

This time I didn't have Mike Pillsbury to soften my fall.

"I don't know how," I whispered to Stacia.

"Yes, you do," she said. "Just like I knew how to listen, you know how to be a hero."

I used to believe I was a hero. But belief is nothing without action. What was the universe screeching at me to believe?

To trust in what I could not see. To try what I could not possibly do.

I tucked my head into a charge position and stormed headfirst at the tree. At the very last moment, I leaped. For a second that lasted a lifetime, I was airborne. The golf cart, the brush, Stacia, and Ditka all disappeared under me. Before me was a tree trunk too fat to hold on to. Above me were tangled branches. I went higher and higher, then reached the top of my jump.

One moment I was flying . . .

Whatever goes up must come down, Pop liked to say.

The next moment I was falling . . .

I lunged at the darkness.

A branch! My arm almost jerked out of the socket but I held on. The branch creaked and I pedaled my feet on the tree, trying to move up. An inch, two inches, then I grabbed the next branch. This one was stronger.

I boosted to the next branch, then the next, until I was into a haze of pine needles. Sap glommed onto my hands; the rough bark cut my stiff palms. I climbed, ignoring the hammering of my heart and the freaking of my brain. Somewhere deep inside, I knew the first leap was the only jump start I would get. The rest was up to me.

The treetop was a maze of branches, as big as any mansion on Stacia's street. How would I ever find the Lyra without Stacia to guide me? She was far below me; I didn't want to yell and alert the Shards.

"Hey, ladybird," I called softly. "Mrs. Lyra?"

Nothing. *She doesn't speak,* I reminded myself. *She communicates through singing.* I didn't know any of Stacia's fancy music. So I whistled "Jingle Bells."

A tiny note tinged above me. I climbed, whistling softly. Another note, and I turned to the left. More notes, and I pushed through a mass of pine tangle. My hand closed on feathers.

The Lyra jumped behind a curtain of branches before I could even see her. The limb shook like an earthquake. She was scared.

"I'm Scott Schreiber. It's okay. Come on out."

She stayed hidden.

"You've been calling for help," I said. "My friend Mike and I heard you. But Stacia, she could understand what you were saying, where to find you." I yodeled it, trying to make it music.

She stayed silent.

"You probably expected a big space guy with muscles and laser guns. Or maybe a genius like Mike Pillsbury or someone wise like Barnabus. I'm sorry I'm not the hero you wanted."

She stayed still.

"But I'm here. That's the best I can do. And I want to help you, more than anything else."

She stayed scared.

"Even more than playing football, I want to help you."

A ball of silver fluff and golden haze pushed from the dark branches. Even in the dark of night, she was perfectly visible. The Lyra carried her own glow with her. Her eyes were the color of sunrise, pale gold with dashes of blues and grays. A fine fuzz, lighter than a kitten's fur, covered her round face. A narrow nose pulled her upper lip into a soft, birdlike beak. Her body was round and small, the size of Mike's neighbor, Little Jay. But her wings were massive, layered with shining silver and gold feathers. Underneath the wings, she had delicate arms, like a child's. And when she uncurled her legs, they were longer and skinnier than Pillsbury's.

She was part bird, part person, all amazing.

"Come on," I hummed. "I'll help you get down."

As she moved closer, the tip of her wing caught on a branch. A broken bone poked out from the feathers on her right side; her face twisted in pain. She twittered to herself and the pain washed from her face.

But the fear stayed.

"It's okay," I whispered. "We have your babies and they're fine."

She smiled, then threw back her head and sang her thanks. Warmth and light sparked in my toes and shot up through me, a lightning bolt of happiness.

Joy, I thought. *Joy to the world.*

18

"YOU OUGHT TO BE IN JAIL, YOU-YOU-"
Pillsbury pummeled at me as I dragged him out of
bed. "You stalker! Get out of my house or I'll call the
cops!"

"This is a legal entry." I laughed. "Your mother
let me in. She's been up since four, making walnut
stuffing and nutmeg squash."

Pillsbury ran into his bathroom and locked the
door. "Go away."

"Don't you want to hear a cool story?"

"You have no right to tell any stories!"

"This story, I do." I jimmied the lock and shoved
my way in. Pillsbury waved a toilet brush in my
face.

"I own the stories!" he snarled.

"Not this story, you don't," I said. "Now, are you

gonna listen or do I have to make you?"

Pillsbury jabbed the brush at my midsection. "Just try it."

"What're you gonna do? Scour me?" I grabbed Pillsbury by the ear and twisted him into the crook of my arm—Ma's favorite wrestling move. Then I forced his head toward the toilet. "You gonna listen?"

"To what? Your egotistical blather? Your ignorant ranting?" Pillsbury's voice was muffled by the porcelain.

"You gonna listen?" I muscled his face closer to the water. Being the Pillsbury house, even the toilet bowl was spotless.

"To what? Your cowardly lies?"

"You gonna listen?" I flushed; water burbled around Pillsbury's head.

Pillsbury sputtered but wouldn't give in. "Why should I? You never listen to me."

The kid had a point. I jerked him out of the toilet. "I'll make you a deal. If you listen to me this time, I swear I'll listen to you next time."

Pillsbury flipped on the faucet and soaked his head in the sink. "Drown me if you want," he bubbled. "But I'm done trusting you."

"Fine. We'll do this the hard way." I slung him over my shoulder and carried him down the stairs, kicking and screaming.

"Enjoy the practice!" Mrs. Pillsbury sang out.

"Call the police, I'm being kidnapped," Pillsbury yelled, wishboning his legs so I couldn't get him through the front door.

"That's nice, dear," his mother called. "Just remember that dinner is at two. Have fun and don't break anything."

I folded Pillsbury sideways and jogged him out the door. I lugged him into the backyard and dumped him under the big elm tree.

"I won't listen." Mike jabbed his fingers into his ears and squeezed his eyes shut.

Pop taught me that a man's whistle sounds like a locomotive coming down the tracks. A man's whistle can shut up a noisy gang of football players or catch the attention of a pretty girl from across the mall parking lot. But even with the weak November sun just coming over the horizon and frost covering the ground, when I man-whistled in Pillsbury's face, it sounded like springtime and fairy bells.

And Mike Pillsbury put down his hands to listen.

The Lyras gave up their home planet to sing their music to the stars. Thousands of races, from the scum-swilling Sluggs to the hotheaded Xgonearks to the wispy Mystics, invited the Lyras to sing on their worlds. The Lyras were pleased to sing for any people of goodwill but swore their friends to secrecy—the

Lyras had learned long ago that some folks refuse to accept the gift of their music.

Though they ordinarily lived in houses, boats, airspheres, or whatever lodging their hosts provided, when it came time to start a family, a Lyra couple had to go to a tree-filled planet so they could build nests and raise hatchlings. One such pair, Lark and Herald, traveled to Centaura, a planet with wide meadows and mighty Harna trees. The Centaurs, mighty creatures with horse legs and human upper bodies, were happy to have Lark and Herald live in their treetops.

Because the Lyras never used machines or tools, someone always had to transport them to a birthing planet. Sometimes the Lyras winged through Bom star gates, sometimes they folded through space warps provided by Lulas, sometimes they chugged along on Jibbs' solar sailboats.

Lark's and Herald's drivers were Ursas. These friendly, hairy folk traveled in space tubs, spinning balls that dipped into gravity wells to make interstellar travel. An Ursan ship brought Lark and Herald to Centaura and promised to return when Lark and Herald's hatchlings were grown. But first these two Lyras had a nest to make, eggs to keep warm, lullabies to sing. The music of the stars could wait.

But the stars refused to wait. The Ursan ship

was detected by their enemy, the Shards. When the Shards seized the ship and learned that they had at last tracked down the object of their quest, they mounted an assault on Centaura. First they sent the disgusting Gargoyle troops to mow down the natives. The Centaurs fought hard to protect their Lyra guests but they were easily overrun by the acid-spouting slime balls.

When the way was clear, the Shards began their hunt for Lark and Herald. Awesome and glowing, the Shards reflected light in a thousand ways. But the light was all on the outside; inside they were disgusting and nasty. Despite the begging of the Centaur prisoners, the Shards ordered the burning of the mighty Harna forests to drive the Lyras out of hiding.

Lark carried the nest in her little arms while Herald flew guard. As the Shards closed in, Herald spotted an Ursan lifeboat entering the planet's atmosphere. Herald shouted up a storm and flew a diversion, allowing Lark to get the nest to a lifeboat that had spun out of the Ursan ship. Even so, there was a bloody battle and the Ursan pilot died to save her.

Lasers ripped open the skies and Herald fell to the ground, his feathers burned and his wings and legs broken. The last Lark heard of him, he sang about his love. She sang her promise to keep his children free to make their own music.

The lifeboat auto-launched into space. Unable to read instruments or navigate the ship, Lark sang her prayers and warmed her eggs. The ship whipped through the gravity wells. Lark had no clue where she might end up, except probably dead.

The Shards finally caught up to the lifeboat as it spun by our own sun. Lark couldn't have surrendered if she'd wanted to—she couldn't figure out how to control the ship or even open the hatch. As the ship cruised by Earth, the Shards blasted the boat out of the sky.

Lark drifted down to Earth. She hid her nest and then flew to the highest tree she could find. As Lark sang for help, she took a blast from a Shard laser and tumbled into the darkness.

And I think you know the rest.

"I know one thing," Pillsbury sputtered. "You're nuts!"

"You don't know everything all the time. Sometimes I know things, too."

"How could you know this?" Pillsbury sneered.

How did I know anything? Screeching, flying, dreaming—sometimes soaring—it all just worked its way into my head. "I didn't ask for this, like you did when you met the Hanzels," I explained. "But even so, I *know*."

"You know crap," Pillsbury said under his breath. I slung him over my shoulder and carried

124

his kicking butt to the tree house.

"You're a dim-witted dolt, an ignorant imbecile, an abysmal blockhead—" Pillsbury cursed me all the way up the ladder. "You're a boneheaded brute, a witless nitwit, a dingbatty dope. You're a—"

We swung into the tree house and, for the first time in his life, words failed Albert Michael Pillsbury. "You're a—a—a—"

"An angel?" I grinned.

"An angel," he whispered.

19

"SHE'S NOT REALLY AN ANGEL," Mike said.

"Duh," I said. "No kidding. She's a Lyra."

"What are you doing with her? Why didn't she come to me? *I'm* the alien expert. I knew all about the Lyras and the Shards before you. Before anyone!"

I bit my tongue to keep from chewing Pillsbury out. Why should he own the universe any more than the rest of us? "She did come to you. You had the game plan . . . you knew the story. It was my job to run with the ball . . . get the nest, get her out of the tree. Stacia called the signals . . . she's the only one who can understand what Lark says. Get it, Pillsbury? Lark needs all of us."

Lark lifted her tiny hand, greeting Mike with a wave and a shy song. He stared at her—no smile, not even a nod of encouragement. She closed her eyes and dipped her head under her good wing.

"Be polite," I whispered. "You're hurting her feelings."

"Polite? You're lecturing me on manners?"

"No, I'm lecturing you on teamwork."

The silence was so long it was painful. Then Mike shook his head and whistled, a wimpy sound—a girl's whistle, Pop would have called it. Lark poked her head back out. Her eyes were wet and dull.

"It's okay," Mike sang, sounding like a strangled cat. "We're all going to help you. This band girl Stacia, Scott, and me."

Lark tipped her head back and warbled.

Mike's face exploded with a silly grin. "You're welcome!"

"So are we cool, Pillsbury?" I asked.

"Absolute zero cool."

The rest of the morning, we fed Lark potato chips and chocolate chip cookies from the stash in the tree house. When that food ran out, we sneaked into the house and grabbed whatever we could find. She ate anything we gave her—from Mrs. Pillsbury's sausage stuffing to Mike's favorite fig bars. And as she munched, she chattered. Sometimes happy, sometimes frightened, she didn't stop her quiet music.

127

Stacia had a command performance at her house for a formal Thanksgiving dinner. "With black tie, china, and politicians," she had moaned. When we brought the injured Lark to Mike's tree house in the middle of the night, Stacia had promised to return later on Thanksgiving Day and bring Lark her eggs.

Around noontime, Ditka showed up at the tree house. Instead of bringing Lark's eggs, he brought bad news. "Guess who came to dinner?" he snarled.

Pillsbury told his parents that he wanted to eat in the woods. "To experience Thanksgiving like the Pilgrims did," he said. They thought it was a great idea and began to pack up the meal so the family and their guests could all join him. Then Mike reminded them they couldn't plug in the espresso machine in the woods.

"Let us know how it goes," his father said, reaching for another cup.

Ma almost ripped my head off. "Your nana is here," she shouted. "Uncle Burt brought pickled newts for an appetizer. What do you mean, you have football practice?"

The lie made my stomach sick. But I couldn't tell Ma about the aliens. No way she'd believe me— she'd go on and on about my head injury and the Caraviellos' evil fence and brutal football. She wouldn't stop to catch a breath, let alone consider that aliens might want their own bird for Thanksgiving—in this case, a Lyra ladybird.

"It's because I missed practice on Monday," I said. "The head injury and the mess-up with the science project. I'll be home for turkey sandwiches at suppertime."

Ma shoved a drumstick into my hand and pushed me out the door. "Be careful, Scottie," she yelled. "No rough stuff."

No rough stuff? How well would Ma's turkey leg hold up against Shard lasers?

Mr. Caraviello slammed the door in our faces. "Scott," he said through the side window, "you know we don't allow dogs in our house."

Ditka growled. "I am not a dog."

"Shh," I whispered. "Mr. Caraviello, he's not a dog . . . he's a . . ."

"Shh," Mike whispered. "You want to get us all neutralized?"

"Shh," I almost shouted, then dropped my voice. "I know what I'm doing, Pillsbury." I leaned into the window. "Mr. Caraviello, he's a seeing-eye dog. You see, my friend Mike Pillsbury, he . . ."

Mr. Caraviello blushed as he opened the door. "Come on in, gentlemen. Sorry about the misunderstanding. So nice of you to join us."

Mike stumbled in, his hand grasping Ditka's

back. Mr. Caraviello pulled me aside. "Scott, if your friend is . . . you know . . . why does he wear glasses?"

"He never gives up hope," I said, trying to keep a straight face. The tie I had borrowed from Pillsbury felt like a noose around my neck. Sweat rolled down my back but froze as soon as I spotted John Cutter across the room.

"Young Schreiber!" he called out. "So nice to see you again."

"Yeah? Well, it's not so nice to see—"

Mike cut me off. "To what do we owe this pleasure, Agent Cutter?"

"The mayor invited me to come along." Cutter smiled at Mr. Caraviello. "I'm here on a project of great environmental urgency. Scott discovered a rare nest and was kind enough to turn it over to my agency for protection."

The Shard dug a finger into my shoulder. "He'll be helping us locate the maker of the nest as well." A pinpoint of blood trickled down my back, under my shirt.

"I'm always happy to help out the authorities," I said, pulling away. "The *proper* authorities, of course."

Stacia was hiding in her music room, having hysterics. "I thought I killed him!" she sobbed. "I hit him with my guitar and he burst into a million pieces. I almost had a heart attack when he walked in with the mayor!"

"It's almost impossible to kill a Shard," Ditka yapped. "Their structure is crystalline, so if they're attacked they can shatter, then re-form."

"So what do we do?" Mike asked.

Stacia wiped her teary hands on her dress, then extended one to Pillsbury. "I'm Stacia Caraviello, by the way," she said. "You must be Mike."

Mike shook her hand. "I've admired your music for a long time. Especially Mozart's Violin Concerto 3 in G Major."

"Oh, thank you," she gushed. "And I've admired your essays in the school newspaper, especially the one on cognitive learning and right-brained—"

"Oh thank you," I mocked. "Just what I needed, a right-brained barf session." The sudden sparkle in Stacia's eyes made me want to pound Pillsbury like a bass drum. "Can we save the culture crap for when we don't have a homicidal alien in the living room?"

"What do we do?" Stacia asked me. "My parents think he's a distinguished guest!"

I looked at Pillsbury. "What?" he cried. "These are your aliens, not mine!"

"You started this," I snapped. "So think."

"It's obvious—we've got to get the eggs out of here."

"Cutter will watch our every move," Ditka said.

"There's one of him and four of us," Mike said. "We'll make a distraction, then get the eggs out of the house and back to Lark. Cutter doesn't know me so he won't be able to track us back to the tree house."

"Where are the eggs?" I asked Stacia.

"In the cupola."

"What's a cupola?" Ditka said, his ears perked.

"That's what Mr. Pillsbury drinks all that Italian coffee in," I said.

Mike punched me. "Don't you ever do your vocabulary homework? A cupola is a small, ornamental structure on the top of a house."

Mrs. Caraviello stuck her head in. "Stacia, the guests are waiting."

"Be right there, Mother."

"Waiting for what?" I asked.

Stacia sighed. "For me to play."

"Oh. Right." Why did I keep forgetting that she was someone special?

Mike pulled us into a huddle. "While Stacia plays, Ditka and I will distract Cutter. Scott, you go up to the cupola and get the eggs. We'll all meet back at my tree house."

Sounded like a plan of attack. I just hoped the Shards didn't have the blitz on.

20

THE CARAVIELLOS' IMPORTANT GUESTS,
all in stiff clothes and shiny shoes, crowded the
living room. Glasses clinked, the fire roared, the
smells of apples and cinnamon filled the air. But as
Stacia lifted her bow everything went away . . . the
people, the Thanksgiving dinner, even John Cutter.

Stacia's violin rang with music—running, leaping, crying, dancing. Her head bobbed as her bow
flew over the strings. No one else moved, but even
so, we were all transported somewhere else.

*Stand in the darkness, listen in the stillness, hold
your gaze on the stars, and you'll hear the music that
stretches across infinity, that binds every possibility
into a wonderful certainty.*

Stacia made the music and the music made
everything right.

A light flashed in the corner of my eye. I tried to blink it away but a sudden fear seized my gut as I remembered why we were there. John Cutter's hair reflected candlelight as he slipped through the dining room and headed for the double doors at the back. The hunt was on.

Come on, Pillsbury, I thought. *Be a good blocker. Give me a hole to slip through.*

As I raced for the stairs, Ditka leaped onto the dining room table. China, silver, and rolls flew everywhere. Mrs. Caraviello screamed, "This is what happens when you let a dog in the house!"

Ditka grabbed the turkey in his mouth and headed in the same direction Cutter had gone. Mr. Caraviello, swinging a golf club, dashed after Ditka. In a minute, John Cutter would be surrounded by a mob of hungry people who wanted their dinner back.

I booked it upstairs. Then up a second flight— this house was huge, with three floors of rooms. Go to the left, Stacia had said, through a small library. When I ducked into the room, I almost drowned in an ocean of books. The Caraviello version of *small* was bigger than my whole house. The stairs—where were the stairs? There, a narrow dark door built into the back shelves.

I hustled up creaky iron steps. The barking from three floors below rocked the walls. It sounded like Ditka didn't know the difference between a distraction and a disaster.

I pushed open a trapdoor and navigated through an attic that was filled with antique furniture, trunks, clothes, skis, wooden sleds. Stacia's footprints in the dust led to a wooden ladder. I climbed twenty more rungs to yet another hatch and opened it to sunlight.

The cupola was a small, dome-shaped glass room perched on the top of the Caraviello mansion. To the north, the flag on top of Ashby Town Hall waved in the afternoon wind. To the west, the mighty trees of Willard Forest covered the horizon.

Above me, the afternoon sun danced on the glass roof. I shaded my eyes and squinted into the glare. No, not sunlight—Shard ships hovered overhead, transparent like dragonfly wings and as deadly as a hawk stalking a mouse.

The eggs sat in their basket, covered with a light blanket. I slid them into the pocket of my football jacket. "Time to go home to your mama," I yodeled, feeling their hum next to my ribs.

"Time to go home, but not to Mama," John Cutter said, popping his head through the trapdoor.

I slammed the hatch on his fingers. *BANG!* My body shuddered as John Cutter threw his shoulder into the wood. He outweighed me by a hundred pounds—it would only be a matter of seconds before he popped me off.

I was on top of the world with no place to go. The roof of Stacia's house was flat all the way to the edges, where it sloped over the attic windows. The nearest tree was twenty or thirty feet away. The ground was four stories below. Even if the fall didn't break me, it certainly would break the eggs.

SLAM! I held on to the sides of the cupola and kept my footing. *SLAM!* I stumbled on one foot. The hatch rose an inch. I stomped it back down. Where was Pillsbury? Why wasn't Ditka up here, chomping on Cutter's butt?

SLAM! I had to make a move, but to where?

SLAM! Cutter jammed his shoulder, then his arm, through the opening. His dagger fingernails flashed in the sun. I jumped again but couldn't close the hatch.

"Hold on, birdies," I whispered into my pocket. "We gotta take an alternate route home."

I rolled out onto the roof. The tiles were slate; I slipped and slid as I ran to the edge. On the lawn far below, Ditka was trapped in a net and roaring mad. Pillsbury jabbered at a policeman, having given up on his blind act.

"Help—" I started to yell.

Cutter's hand over my mouth cut off my cries. "Give me the eggs."

I elbowed his gut. His stomach splintered and he went down on one knee. I waved and hollered at Pillsbury but Ditka's barking drowned me out. Cutter was up again. He raced after me, then slipped on the slate. I had just a few seconds before he'd be up yet again. Where could I go?

If I could fly *up*, maybe I could fly *down*. Did I dare risk the eggs by leaping off the roof? I had no choice. I climbed partway up a chimney, closed my eyes, and stepped off.

I crashed to the slate. Why couldn't I fly? And then I realized, maybe I never really flew. Maybe my out-of-this-world ability was something that wasn't quite flying. Maybe something more like jumping. Really *far* jumping.

Cutter walked slowly across the roof. His hair gleamed like diamonds and his face reflected the sunlight; he looked like a knight in shining armor. But I wasn't fooled—this dude had a black hole where his heart should be.

Now or never, Thirteen.

I took a running start and hurdled off the roof. The ground whizzed below me as I pedaled over empty space. *A little farther, please, just a little farther.* WHAMP! I hit a massive tree limb. I grabbed and kicked, crashing downward until I tumbled onto a branch that would hold me.

As I shinnied down the rest of the tree, I took deep breaths. *The eggs are safe,* I told myself. *The eggs are safe.*

But Stacia wasn't. John Cutter waited outside the front gate, one hand clutched around Stacia's wrist, the other around her violin. Stacia's knees wobbled, but each time she slumped Cutter yanked her up.

"You butthole," I said. "Leave her alone."

"Fine. Give me the eggs," Cutter said.

"Eggs? What eggs?" I asked, trying to keep my voice light. "I was just out for a walk."

Mike appeared at my shoulder. "Oh, no," he whispered. "No."

"Oh, yes," John Cutter snarled. "Tell your comrade to give me the eggs."

"What eggs?" Mike asked, his eyes wide. "Oh, you mean those delicious deviled eggs the Caraviello's chef made?" His glasses reflected John Cutter as a haze of sparkles. "They were quite excellent."

"What glasses?" Cutter laughed, ripping Mike's glasses off his face and crushing them in his hand. Stacia tried to slip away but Cutter grabbed her back. "Tell them to give me the eggs."

"What eggs?" she said, her eyes blinking tears the size of blueberries.

"What eggs? Let's rephrase that, shall we? What *fingers?*" Cutter jerked Stacia's hand over her head. His razor claws shone in the afternoon sun. "These fingers?" He poked Stacia's thumb and a tiny drop of blood oozed out.

"No!" I leaped for him. Pillsbury jumped on my back.

"He'll take your head off," he hissed.

138

"Let him try it, the goose-bellied, Bom-faced, son of a Loapher," I said, swinging wildly, half at Cutter and half at Pillsbury.

"I'm not going to take your head off, young Schreiber," Cutter said. "Not this time. However, this young lady who makes such marvelous music is about to lose her fingers. Unless you care to trade them for those eggs."

"No, Scott, don't," she whimpered. "Even this creep wouldn't do such a horrible thing."

"Don't be deceived," Mike gasped. "He's done more disgusting evil than we can imagine."

"What will it be, young Schreiber?"

I slowly pulled the eggs out of my pocket and held them to my cheek. "I'm so sorry. We'll get you back," I promised.

Stacia collapsed in tears as Cutter sped away with her violin, Pillsbury's broken glasses, and Lark's babies.

The eggs' terrified screech hung in the air long after Cutter's car had disappeared.

21

STACIA CROUCHED IN A CORNER OF THE tree house, her eyelashes flapping like flags in a high wind. Pillsbury squinted continuously, now near-blind for real without his glasses. Ditka whined and snorfled, his head hidden under his massive paws. Pop had bailed him out of the dog pound, fed him three pounds of turkey, then let him out to *play* with us. "Cheer him up," Pop said. "He looks kinda sad."

Sad? I felt like I had been dipped in cold cement, so deep was the sadness that weighed me down.

Lark's cries of pain and fear rocked Pillsbury's neighborhood. Mike's parents sat on the front steps and bawled their eyes out. "Thanksgiving is so special," his mother sobbed.

"Then why are we so miserable?" Mr. Pillsbury sputtered back.

Little Jay from next door hid in the toolshed. "There's bogeymen around," he called to his weepy parents. Up and down the street, people stumbled out of houses, dabbing their eyes, blinking back pain and fear. How had such a bright Thanksgiving day gone so bad?

"The power to persuade," Mike explained. "Everyone in the neighborhood is picking up Lark's agony."

My heart couldn't break into any more pieces. "You've got to stop it," I yelled at her. Lark kicked at me with her long legs but I danced away. Then she flapped her good wing and knocked me so hard that I stumbled and fell out of the tree house.

I was flat on my back, frozen to the hard ground. This was how it had all begun. Was it all over for good? Or, in this case, for very, very bad?

Above me, Lark barged past Mike, a storm of feathers and shrieks. She lifted her shoulders, perched in the door of the tree house, and launched herself into the air.

One moment I flew.

She screamed in agony as she tried to raise her broken wing. It bent like a busted wishbone. Lark's good wing beat wildly, flipping her in circles. She couldn't hold the air current and spun toward the ground.

The next moment I fell.

Like a pass tottering out of the sky, I caught the

Lyra as she plunged to the ground. She was surprisingly light, but as I held her she pounded me with her little fists, determined to fly again.

Mike and Stacia jostled down the ladder. "Tell her to calm down," I said, trying to restrain her without hurting her.

"She can't bear it," Stacia sobbed. "She lost Herald and now she's lost her children."

She lost Herald—something tumbled in my brain but I couldn't catch it. "It's my fault she lost the eggs," I said.

"Snakes and snails! She hasn't lost them, not yet," Ditka said. We followed his snout skyward. The Shard ships lingered overhead.

"Why are they hanging around? They got what they wanted," I said.

"Maybe they want more now. Maybe they've decided they like Earth," Ditka snarled. "With three Lyras in their control, the sky is the limit. And to them, this backward planet would be easy pickings."

"Wait a minute!" Mike yelped. "Those eggs haven't even hatched yet. They can't make anyone do anything."

"It's only a matter of days," Ditka warned.

"But meanwhile, we have a full-grown Lyra who just turned my whole neighborhood into mush."

"You got a play to call, Pillsbury?" I asked.

"Maybe . . . yeah, it might work. Stacia, tell Lark we're going to get her babies back and make those Shards go away for good," Pillsbury said.

Stacia sang high notes and warbled a whistle or two. Lark answered her with a low song. A strange peace settled over us all. Lark believed we could do it, so we believed we could do it. The question was: What exactly were we going to do?

"We'll mount an invasion," Pillsbury said.

"With what air force?" I choked.

Mike smiled. "You."

"Are you nuts?" I screamed. "What am I gonna do, tackle a fleet of spaceships?"

"Just one," Ditka said, wagging his tail. "The command ship. That's where John Cutter will be."

"And what will those twenty other ships be doing while I'm tackling John Cutter? Who, I remind you, has threatened to *cut off my head!*"

Mike smoothed Lark's feathers. Her golden eyes glowed as if she could read his mind. I didn't have a clue what he was getting at.

"They'll be listening to music," he said.

"I thought you were a hero," Pillsbury said.

"A hero, yes. A suicidal maniac? Not in a million years," I moaned. Ditka chomped on my leg, trying to pull me out of the tree house. "I'm not doing it."

"Okay, then," Mike said. "I'll do it."

143

"You're too skinny," Stacia cried. "I'll do it—my arms are strong!"

"You can't risk injury," Mike argued.

"Like playing the violin is going to matter if the Shards take over our planet?"

"Why don't we use the Sirian's ship?" I snapped. "This is his operation, after all."

Ditka chased his tail. "It's a cheap piece of trash— not a military fighter. They'd see it coming and flick it out of the sky like a flea. I do have a small trans- porter gate—but it's not a fancy all-in-one model like the Boms use. Before we can use it, someone needs to set up the receiving end. Up there."

"I said I would do it," Stacia said.

"Stacia, this isn't exactly in your realm of expe- rience," Mike argued.

"Hey, how much more experienced do I have to get? I let a dog in my house. I carjacked my father's golf cart. I ruined Thanksgiving dinner with the mayor and the governor. I might as well disobey big time and leave the planet."

"Shut up!" I yelled. "Just shut up! We all know I'm going to do this. Just give me a minute, okay? Everyone just get OUT!"

Stacia, Mike, and Ditka left the tree house. Lark had stayed on the ground, eating lettuce to prepare for our armed assault. Some assault—a broken lady- bird and a wannabe hero, taking on the nastiest dudes in the universe.

Review the game plan, Thirteen. The X's and O's.
The X's were a fleet of spaceships equipped with lasers and razor-sharp troops. There was only one O—me—and I prayed I wouldn't be a big zero. They had power. We had surprise. They had the eggs. We had a mother who would die to save them.

Like my mother, I suddenly realized. Sure, she drove me crazy with her yelling and hovering and smothering. But let John Cutter flash those dagger hands at me and I knew that she wouldn't even hesitate—Ma would give him the haircut of his life. There was no force in the universe stronger than a mom looking out for her kid.

I had nothing to be afraid of.

"Oh heck, I'm gonna pee my pants!" I moaned. "Stacia, don't look."

"Will you stop it!" Mike yelled as he fastened the bungee cords around my biceps and forearms. Lark, light as her feathers but powerful as my fear, sat on my back. She calmly allowed Mike to strap her wings to my arms so I could provide the support needed for her busted wing. "You've been into this flying thing for days now."

"It's jumping, not flying. I jumped twenty feet. From a rooftop to a treetop. But those ships are two, three miles up there."

"You can do it, Scott," Stacia said. "Tell him, Lark."

As Lark murmured in my ear, a galaxy of heroes marched past me: conquering rocky planets and blazing stars; quieting angry seas and roaring winds; calming terrified children and paranoid natives. And then Ashby scarlet roared by: Keras, LeSieur, Tenore, Coach Tremblay urging us on. Pillsbury, playbook in hand, stars in his eyes, dreams in his head. I brought up the rear—ready to face any front line, eat any dirt, pound my body for the sake of glory.

Ashby glory. Lyra eggs. Mother Earth. Galactic peace. The universe got bigger and bigger as my heart rose to meet the challenge.

"What're we gonna do?" Mike whispered in my ear.

"WIN!" I bellowed.

22

LARK THREW BACK HER HEAD AND
shouted. I lifted my arms and her broken wing lifted
with me. I lowered, lifted, lowered, lifted, then leapt
into the air.

One moment we flew. And we kept flying!

We rose over the rooftops of Pillsbury's neighborhood, over Ashby Center. The town was dry and
dead for the winter, except the football field—bright
green from water and fertilizer, still spruced up for
a season that hadn't ended.

Roads and houses disappeared under a wisp
of clouds, then reappeared, tiny strings and blocks
on a game board. As we went higher, mountains
melted into hills and lakes pooled in puddles.
Too high—my legs kicked, trying to find solid
ground. But my arms beat on, giving Lark's

wings the support she needed to lift us.

We burst into a cloud bank and the world went white and icy cold. More clouds, then the sky exploded, clear and blue. The Shard fleet barely caught the light; the clear ships were more sky than metal, but like John Cutter's flashy looks, the glitter was all just a fake. A ruse, Pillsbury would say.

Ditka had drilled us about which ship to approach. "The one in the middle; it'll look like a diamond with lots of facets." Sure enough, as we whizzed past the slender ships of the outer fleet, the command ship glimmered in the center of the formation. I held what little breath I had left in the thin air, expecting to be cut to shreds by lasers. The sky was frigid but quiet; Ditka had promised their sensors wouldn't pick up weaponless life-forms.

In other words, a seventh-grade quarterback and a singing alien with a broken wing.

I tilted left and Lark slowed her wings. The command ship threw light like those rotating balls that twirl from the ceiling at school dances. We drifted over the thousand surfaces, my eyes aching from the bouncing reflections, my body shaking from the cold. We needed to get inside, quick. But what does a door to a spaceship look like?

There, on the upper side, a dark ramp. I dipped my right shoulder and Lark moved us in close.

"Okay, Ladybird," I yodeled. "Time to drop by and pay our disrespect."

We tumbled onto the ramp. As I unstrapped the bungees and lowered Lark from my back, I peeked back over the edge. My knees buckled; two hours ago I had thought the roof of Stacia's house was puking high. This was unreal—Earth stretched below us like a blue-and-cloud-speckled sea, like those satellite pictures on the weather forecast.

The winds were fierce; breathing was tense. I grabbed Lark's good wing and steered her toward the door. We had to get inside before we froze from the cold or suffocated in the thin air. Shiny black, the door didn't exactly have a knob or doorbell.

What the heck. I knocked.

The port slid open. A lady Shard, bigger and shinier than John Cutter, stuck a weapon in our faces. I raised my hand and grinned. "Hi, there." Her finger tightened on what had to be the trigger.

"Sing," I whispered to Lark, watching my life pass before me for the third time that week. Lark warbled and whistled and hummed. The Shard squinted. Then her face relaxed and her eyes drooped. As she lowered her weapon, she smiled. She slumped to the floor, drowsy-eyed. Within seconds, she was snoring. First down completion!

But the end zone was still light-years away.

* * *

Pillsbury, Ditka, and Stacia took the easy way up. "How come I didn't get to use the transporter?" I moaned as they passed through the mini-gate that Lark and I had flown to the Shard ship.

"We needed you to set up the receiving end," Ditka growled. "At least you got to take the scenic route." While Stacia and Lark hummed a few bars to get the plan straight, we stuffed chewing gum in our ears to shield us from Lark's persuasive powers. Then we headed into the main chambers of the ship to find the eggs. The halls were a maze of mirrors, turning left, right, up and down, a fairyland of light.

"Wow, it's beautiful," mouthed Stacia.

"Don't be fooled," Mike said. "Look closer."

I pressed my face to a wall. At first it was like staring into the sun. Then my eyes focused past the reflective surface. "The engine room," Mike guessed as we looked at grinding gears and glowing reactors.

Down the hall a little, we peeked again. Troopers stood around a high table, eating. "Maybe they're celebrating their own Thanksgiving," Stacia said. Then she hiccuped with fright. Tiny creatures like mice scurried around the table as the Shards speared them and swallowed them, whole and kicking.

We pulled the gum out of our ears so we could hear each other. "Barbarians," Ditka snarled.

"No race with advanced space travel can be termed barbaric," Mike said.

"Okay. So how about slime hogs, then?" I said, popping the gum back in.

We swung around a corner and ran smack into a guard. Before he could raise his weapon, Ditka clamped his jaws on the guy's wrist. We watched in gross fascination as the Shard's arm shattered, then recrystallized. Meanwhile, Lark sang. Before his hand even finished healing, the Shard was sound asleep.

Down every long hall, around every corner, we ran into Shards. Ditka growled them into submission while Lark sang them to sleep.

"It's like Tchaikovsky's Sleeping Beauty," Stacia said. "The soldiers falling into slumber throughout the palace as they fall under the spell."

"More like FitzSpud's science class," I said. "Being bored into snoozeville."

Pillsbury jabbed my ribs. "Shut up. This is too easy. There's something wrong."

"We got the secret weapon," I boasted. "Cutter wanted Lark but we've got her. They can't stop us. Come on!"

Pillsbury yanked me back. "Stop," he hissed. Ditka froze, his nose in the air, his ears flat.

"What?" I hissed back. Mike's pasty face reflected off the walls, looking so sick that puke rose in my own throat.

"Too easy," Mike whispered. "The eggs aren't any

use to John Cutter, not for a long time. They've got to hatch, grow, learn to sing, be trained to serve the Shards. But Lark . . ." Mike turned bile green. "We made a mistake . . . by bringing Lark here, we've put all our eggs in one basket."

"You put all your eggs in *my* basket." Cutter's voice came from behind us. "For which I thank you, and may let you live."

We all turned. Lark stood like stone. John Cutter held a laser to her head. "Easy, wasn't it? I made it that way." He sneered. "Couldn't have you fail now, could I? Not when I needed the mother so badly."

Lark swung her good wing around and slapped Cutter against the wall. The laser slid across the floor but before I could pounce on it, a Shard trooper recovered it. Lark hopped at Cutter, batting him into shimmering pieces. Moments later, he recrystallized and she batted him again.

"This is getting tedious," he said. He flicked out his claws. Lark cried in hideous pain and all of us— Shards included—felt the sting of Cutter's daggers as he sliced her good wing.

I rolled out of a haze of agony, trying to get to Lark. She sang softly, trying to ease her pain, trying to calm John Cutter. The other Shards quieted but Cutter stood firm and cruel, as if he could resist her song.

"You'll sing for me!" he ordered. "Not for these miserable Earthlings!"

She shrieked a fierce note. No translation was necessary—*drop dead, you skuzzball!*

Cutter reached into a pouch and brought out Lark's eggs. Her eyes widened and she shrieked again. Her grief ripped through my chest as Cutter closed his fist over the eggs, slowly squeezing.

The shells creaked.

"No!" Stacia cried. "They're not ready!"

"Silence!" Cutter snapped. "Do you agree, Lyra?"

Lark closed her mouth and dropped her head.

Cutter put his hand in front of her eyes, tightening his fingers. "I said, do you agree, Lyra?" Lark dropped to her knees and bent her neck in surrender. Stacia cried as Lark allowed Cutter to wrap a muzzle around her beak.

When Lark was silenced, Cutter handed her the eggs. They hummed with delight, not understanding what miserable danger we were all in. Tears dampened the fuzz on Lark's face, then plopped onto her feathered chest, now heaving with sadness.

But she couldn't make a sound now that she was muzzled.

Cutter turned to the rest of us, singling out Pillsbury first. "You think you're so smart." He sneered. "But you were just smart enough to hand-deliver the Lyra to me. And what's this, a disgusting do-gooding Sirian?" He jabbed Ditka's side with the laser. "Always poking their slimy noses where

153

they're not wanted." Ditka showed his teeth but backed away.

As Cutter turned on us, I put my arm around Stacia. "The football hero and his little fiddler friend. Playing boys' games on a man's turf. Well, young Schreiber, as they say in your silly sport—you are about to be benched."

"You scum-sucking, sewer-snorting, manure-mouthed slime bucket!" I cursed. "No one benches the Mighty Schreiber!"

Until now.

23

i BURiED MY FACE iN THE SHREDDED
remains of Lark's nest and cried my heart out.

If the slugs from Bristol could see the un-stoppable Schreiber now—locked in a cell, lying on the floor, sobbing in dirty straw and sparkling strands—they'd laugh their stinky garlic brains out. Cutter had ripped my beautiful nest open in front of me, his dagger hands slicing like a buzzsaw.

Then Cutter had turned to Stacia. He had stolen her violin, a priceless instrument, worth even more in practice and playing time. He broke it in two, then sliced through the strings. "Your pathetic world is falling apart," he said with a sneer, tossing Mike's broken glasses at him. As the door locked with a thud, we collapsed in our private corners.

Stacia cradled her broken violin, her back heaving with sobs. Ditka rolled his huge body into a tight ball and buried his head in his ribs. "When all else fails, they send me," he muttered. "And now I've failed." Pillsbury leaned his head against the wall, rocking slowly. All his thinking wouldn't save us now.

Nick Thorpe's voice pounded in my head. *Hey, guys, look at this*—snort, snort—*the Mighty Schreiber sacked himself!*

I had tried to fly and fell lower than I could even imagine.

Focus, Thirteen. If you're breathing, then the game ain't over. Think: X's and O's. The X's had the lasers, the Lyras, the will to do evil at any cost. The O's were three kids and a whining Sirian locked in a cell. My throat clenched. I rubbed the tears so hard that I saw stars—not Shard ships, but fire. *All flash and no fire*, Pillsbury had said.

He was wrong. No one benched the Mighty Schreiber.

"KILL!" I yelled, and leaped against the door. The room clanged as the metal walls shook. *So this is what it's like without blockers and pads*, I thought as every bone in my body jarred.

"KILL!" I yelled and charged again, my shoulder down, my legs pumping. The door bent, then snapped back into shape.

Click! The door slid open and a Shard guard marched in. The door locked immediately behind her.

She took in the room—Stacia rocking her violin, Ditka hiding in the corner, Mike leaning on the wall, me in a three-point stance, dripping sweat, my stitches leaking blood. Ready for the third-down charge.

She turned her weapon on me. "You have been deemed disposable, young Schreiber. This is your final warning. One more incident and—" The Shard drew her finger across her shining throat.

Click. The door reopened with a *whoosh* and she left. The door shut in a flash, before I got a chance to leap through. Enraged, I dipped my head, pointed my shoulder, and charged. *"Scott Schreiber is not disposable!"*

Pillsbury took me down before I hit the wall.

"Get off me!" I screamed, clawing for the door.

"You'll get yourself killed!" he yelped, holding my legs.

"We have to do something!"

I scrambled up, ready to blast the door again. Then I caught the look in Mike's eyes. Half blind, glasses gone, nevertheless, Pillsbury stared for a long moment, then squinted at me. Something had become very clear in that very weird mind of his.

"We will do something, Thirteen. And I know exactly what."

* * *

"This is nuts," Stacia moaned.

"Everyone says that about Pillsbury," I assured her. "It'll work."

"You could get hurt," she whispered. "Even die. And it would be all my fault!"

"Now you sound like my ma." I laughed. My knees buckled but I willed my legs tight. *Show no fear*, Coach always said. But Coach Tremblay had never faced a Shard laser.

Pillsbury huddled us up. "Put half the gum in your ears and give me the other half." I dragged mine out of my jacket pocket, covered with lint and dirt. Stacia carefully unwrapped hers from the foil. Ditka pawed the ground.

"What?" Pillsbury said.

"I swallowed mine."

Pillsbury rolled his eyes. "Okay, we'll make do. Stacia, are you ready?"

"Mike, this won't work."

"This has to work," he said. "We have no other choice."

"I can't," she said. Her hands trembled but her eyes were stunned to unblinking.

"You can," I said, rubbing her fingers. This hand-holding with a Weird Band Girl had become a habit. "Stacia, you can do it. You make the music."

Her hands quieted as she gave me a tiny, teary smile. She slid the violin under her chin. Pillsbury

158

had helped her repair it using the medical tape from my bandaged neck to stick it back together. We used the strands from Lark's shredded nest to form strings.

"They're not in tune," Stacia worried.

"The fiddle will make its own tune," I said. "Just play."

She put the bow to the violin. The strands sounded like bells on a merry-go-round. We all stuffed the gum back in our ears.

"Keep playing," Mike mouthed with a nervous smile. Then he turned to me, gave me a big thumbs-up. "KILL!"

Or be killed . . . I pushed that thought far down into my belly. No time for cowards now. I leaped for the door. Again and again, crunching my bones, making that metal bend. *"No one benches Scott Schreiber!"* I bellowed.

Click. The guard stepped in and raised her laser. "Stupid Earth boy," she said. Light exploded in my face. *THUMP!* The ceiling split in two! The Shard slumped to the floor, her laser blasting upward. Ditka rushed over and disarmed her.

"She's not asleep," Stacia cried. "I can't make the music Lark made!"

"Good enough," Ditka yelped. "She's laughing her fool head off." The Shard rolled on the floor, twitching and huffing as if some invisible hand

159

was tickling every funny bone in her body.

The door gaped wide open. Pillsbury had shoved chewing gum in the mechanism so it couldn't auto-lock.

"Come on, team," I yelled. "Ain't nothing left in life but Lark and her eggs. Let's go get 'em."

24

THE SCUM SUCKER HAD LOCKED LARK

and her eggs in a cage like dirty animals. The cage hung from the ceiling, suspended like a canary but this ladybird couldn't sing, not with the muzzle still on. Her hands and feet were bound tightly so she had to nestle her eggs under her broken wings. Even with the gum blocking my ears, their screech rattled my brain. How humiliating, to treat the treasure of the universe like a dirty pigeon.

Unable to speak, Lark's eyes spoke for her—for the first time ever, a Lyra wanted to kill.

Stacia had fiddled all the other Shards out of commission. They had chuckled and giggled and guffawed themselves into nausea and then unconsciousness. But as we crept into the control room on our bellies, I feared John Cutter wouldn't have a sense of humor.

"Play," Mike motioned. Stacia slumped behind a heavy console and put the fiddle under her chin. She drew her bow. Through the chewing gum, I dimly heard the music and swallowed the urge to giggle. Cutter was twenty feet away, his back to us. He bent over a glass panel, pushing bright crystals and checking flashing star maps.

Clueless.

"Louder," I mouthed.

Stacia bore down on the strings. The purple, gold, and silver strings sparked under her bow. My belly rumbled with laughter and my cheeks puffed, trying to keep it in.

Cutter just kept working.

Lark turned our way. Her golden eyes smiled and her cheeks twitched, trying to sing with Stacia. The eggs stopped screeching and twinkled along. But John Cutter just kept working.

Mike poked me, then clapped his hands over his ears.

"What?" I shrugged silently.

He clapped his ears again. "The creep is wearing earphones," he mouthed.

"The heck with this," I said. I climbed onto the console and leaped across the room. *BAM!* Cutter went down, shattering under my tackle. In an instant, the crystals re-formed and his muscles bulged back, bigger than ever. As he staggered up, I wrapped my arms around his neck. He bucked me like a wild horse. "Disposable, young Schreiber!" he roared.

He twisted and slammed me into a wall. The shock rattled my backbone but I hung tight. Cutter waved his hands over his head, batting at me. I held on. Across the room, Stacia dropped her patched violin and screamed. "Keep playing!" I yelled.

Ditka grabbed Cutter's leg in his teeth but Cutter kicked him across the room. Mike knocked against Cutter, a rag doll battering a stone wall. Cutter punched Mike, bouncing him silly.

The claws came out. Still holding tight, I arched back, trying to get out of reach. The finger-daggers were too long; he slashed me on the forehead. Blood poured into my eyes and I dimly heard Stacia still screaming. "You gotta play!" I yelled. "It's the only way." Through the crimson curtain, I saw her put the violin back to her chin and lift the bow.

Now or never, Thirteen. Make your play. I let go with one hand, knowing I only had a split second before Cutter tossed me off his back. I groped his head. My fingers closed over an earpiece. As Cutter flung me across the room, I took his earphones with me.

He stomped toward me, staring death. "Keep playing!" I shouted, spitting my own blood. I backed into a corner, knowing my life could flash before me only so many times before the show closed for good.

163

Cutter stepped over Pillsbury, snarling. Ditka leaped for his throat and Cutter one-handed him, cursing. Cutter reached for me, his face twisted with hate. "Young Schreiber . . ." He sneered.

"You have been deemed . . ."

And then he giggled.

Cutter's face split with a happy-go-lucky, let's-party smile. He stumbled around, confused. Then he took in deep gasps of air, trying to stop the laughter. "You have been deemed amusing," he twittered.

"Keep playing!" I yelled.

Stacia fiddled on, tapping her foot, bobbing her head, and smiling up a storm. *This must be what's deep inside her,* I realized. *Quiet peace comes from the Lyra but fun and happiness comes from this Weird Band Girl.*

Cutter slapped his knee, then danced a jig. His eyes sparkled and he twirled, his own private joke sending him spinning.

I wiped the blood out of my eyes just in time to see Ditka leap across the room and knock Cutter on his back. Even with those mighty chompers locked on his throat, Cutter couldn't stop laughing.

What the heck. I loosened one of my gum ear-plugs and laughed with him.

Stacia fiddled like the Pied Piper as Mike and I led the dancing guards into a new cell—one that

164

wasn't impaired with a chewing gum lock. Meanwhile, back in the control room, Ditka stood guard while the unmuzzled Lark sang Cutter to surrender.

One Shard ship down. Twenty to go. "Now what?" I asked Pillsbury when we were back in the control room. "We can't assault every ship like this."

The command console blinked and buzzed. "Bricks and bats! When this ship doesn't respond, they'll realize it is out of commission," Ditka yowled. "They'll be here in a flash. Or worse, they'll suspect a counterassault and turn their lasers on Earth."

"Our families," Stacia cried. "They're down there, helpless!"

Ma would be at the sink now, cleaning up the mess from Thanksgiving. In the fridge, there would be a platter the size of a rowboat for my supper, filled with turkey and gravy and every good thing. Ma would wipe the suds from her arms, check on Pop in front of the TV, then go out and stand on the front steps. Without a coat, not minding the cold—she would wait for me to come back from football practice.

"What can we do?" Ditka howled.

"Why don't these losers just get lost!" I snapped.

"Schreiber!" Mike yelled. "You're a genius!"

"Don't make fun of me!"

"I'm not! It's a brilliant plan!" Mike said. "Stacia, tell Lark we need her to sing one more song." Mike fiddled with Cutter's crystal panel. Lights flickered, reflecting red, blue, and yellow on Pillsbury's face.

A voice echoed out of the walls. "Ship One, what is your command?"

Pillsbury grabbed what looked like a mike. "Hold for instructions," he said, roughing his voice to sound Shard-strong. He pressed his hand over the speaker portion. "Lark, we need you to broadcast to all the ships."

Lark hiccuped short notes. Stacia translated. "She doesn't know what to say."

"Tell them to go home!" I yelped.

"That won't do any good," Ditka snapped. "They'll just turn around and come back. Shards don't give up easily."

"Schreiber got it right the first time. They've got to get lost," Mike said. "We need to send them on a goose chase so wild that they'll never come back."

Stacia shook her head. "She says she's a simple singer—she can't make a song that complicated. The song would have to—" Lark whistled and Stacia translated. "The song would have to be like a story to stick with them, a story they believed in."

"Ticks and fleas," Ditka cursed. "We need a story-teller."

"Ice cream and candy!" I laughed. "We've got the best storyteller in the world. Heck, in the whole universe!"

25

THE SHARDS WERE THE MOST MAR-
*velous people in the universe. Whatever they wanted,
they got; and that was only fair. There was no race or
species or creature greater than the amazing Shards
of Pavo. They deserved to have forever every good
thing.*

I whacked Mike in the shoulder. "What're you
doing? Kissing up to these scum?"

"Trust me," he whispered. "First we catch their
attention. Then we bag these buzzards." As Mike
told the story, Lark sang it. Ditka had set the command ship's communications system to broadcast
her song to the whole fleet. John Cutter, with no
restraints or chains, sat quietly at Lark's feet, listening to his new future unfold.

Because the Shards were so great and wonderful,

so handsome and beautiful, so intelligent and wise, so gracious and giving . . .

"Pillsbury, you're making me gag." I choked. He whacked me, then continued the biggest buttkissing in the history of the universe.

The Wise Counsel had posed the Great Question: "What is the meaning of All This?" The Shards declared they were the only people worthy to answer the question. They announced that they would undertake a mission to find the beginning of All This.

"How will you do that?" the Dough Boy asked.

"We will travel forever if we must," the valiant Shards swore. "We will fly to the center of all matter, we will fly to the end of the charted universe, we will sweep every galaxy in between. All This must have a beginning and All This must have an end. . . . WE will find the beginning so WE can know the end.

My head spun. I looked at John Cutter, afraid he would leap down Pillsbury's throat and slice him silly. But the Shard's eyes dimmed, those crystal flashes now a sputter of confused sparks. "Find the beginning," he whispered.

Pillsbury grinned.

"Find the beginning," the Shards vowed, on the honor of all edges bright and sharp. "We will not return until we have mastered the beginning and beheld the end. But how do we begin to search the beginning?"

"You must have a plan," the Weird Girl of Band advised them. *"Gather your formidable fleet and first speed to the heart of this galaxy. If the beginning is not there, spiral outward. Search every star system, every quasar cloud, every pulsing gas mass."*

"We can do it!" the Shards swore. *"We will do it!"*

Lark's eyes laughed as she sang. Ditka kept his nose on business—his teeth bared at Cutter's throat in case the Shard made one false move.

Cutter smiled and nodded and clapped with delight—with the help of Albert Michael Pillsbury and Lark the Lyra, the Shard saw his heroic path shining before him and was ready to jump on board.

Only one question remained. My team would follow me into a snake-infested swamp; would Cutter's fleet follow him to the beginning of All This and back?

"And how will we know the beginning of All This when we find it?" John Cutter asked.

Pillsbury's face went blank. *"Uh . . ."*

Ditka leaned his massive snout into Pillsbury's ear. Pillsbury's grin returned.

The Master of Bones decrees these signs. When tails wag up and down, instead of side to side. When the blitz is made of chocolate and a sack is filled with blitzes. When X's-and-O's and sharps-and-flats and ticks-and-fleas live in perfect harmony. When white is black and black is crystal clear. When a first down lasts forever and summer vacation lasts

*even longer. When every song is sweeter than the
last.*

"When may we start?" John Cutter asked,
bouncing excitedly like a kid about to open birthday
presents.

"Now! The Mighty Thirteen decrees," I shouted.

Ditka shook his head. Pillsbury gave me the cut
sign. As he conferred with Ditka, his face drained of
color. "No!" he hissed, looking back at me like I was
a ghost.

"Someone's got to do it," Ditka said in a low
growl. "Or they'll track right back to Earth."

"Do what?" I yelped. But Mike closed his eyes and
resumed the story. His voice went flat and, even as
Lark sang, the fun was somehow gone from his story.

*The Mighty Thirteen decrees that you begin your
journey once your fleet is clear of extraterrestrials.
This is a Shard mission and it is only fitting that
Shards alone undertake this search. While you plot
your course to the center of this galaxy, the Counsel
will clear all undesirables and unworthies from
your ship. You will then be issued the signal "Seek!"
and you may begin.*

Is this clear, Cutter?

John Cutter sparked to attention. His eyes
swirled clear crystal once more but he looked right
through us, as if setting his sights on something
bigger and better. "Clear," he said.

170

Please confirm with your fleet.

Ditka nodded to Stacia, who passed the microphone to Cutter. As Cutter spoke, Stacia crossed her fingers.

We held our breaths as the confirmation from each ship came in. If even one pilot was not persuaded by Lark's song, we would be looking down the kicking end of a laser. Ship 1 came on-line, ready to receive the flight plan. Ship 2, Ship 3. Then a hesitation from Ship 4. I knew we'd been found out. But no, Ship 4 had its own suggestions about finding the beginning of All This. Ships 5 and on answered, ready to obey. But it wasn't until Ship 20 clicked in that we all breathed again.

"Wise Counsel, please clear the ship of extraterrestrials. We will launch on your signal." Cutter turned back to his console, plotting his course to nowhere.

No one needed to be told twice—we were out of the control room, through the corridors, and at the exit before you could say "pass interference."

I flipped the switch on Ditka's transporter gate. "Stacia first," I said, and scooted her to the gate.

Lark warbled something and Stacia paused. "She wants me to take the eggs."

Pillsbury twittered and squirmed with an I'm-not-gonna-give-bad-news-to-anyone look. "What!" I yelled.

171

"Nothing," he said. "Stacia, take them. They'll be safer if you carry them than if Lark tries to. She needs her hands to keep her broken wings from flopping around."

Stacia took the eggs from Lark, then kissed Lark's cheek. "See you in a few seconds," Stacia said. She stepped toward me and I thought for a moment she would kiss me. Then she blinked her eyes rapidly and stepped through, eggs in one hand, violin in the other.

"Lark," I said, motioning Lark forward.

No one moved.

"What!" I yelled. "What is the big hairy deal here?" Someone was going to get a serious kick if I didn't get an answer.

"We have a problem," Ditka barked. "Stacia didn't need to know about it."

Pillsbury spoke so softly I had to strain to hear the bad news. "Ditka's transporter gate . . . if we all go through back to Earth, one end would be on the Shard ship. No matter how lost the Shards got, they would always be able to find their way back to us."

The realization swept through me, a mighty fist whacking me into next week. Someone needed to stay behind to destroy the transporter.

"I'll do it," Ditka said.

"You can't," Mike argued. "You've still got to

contact the Ursas and arrange transport for Lark and the eggs. I'll stay."

"You?" I asked.

"Why not?"

"They'll swallow you in a second."

"Not necessarily. I'm smart. Resourceful," he argued. "I'll destroy the transporter, then stay out of their sight until they land at a friendly planet." His voice trailed off. "My parents . . . Katelyn . . . tell them . . ."

"You tell them," I snarled. "I brought the transporter gate here and I'll do the job of getting rid of it."

"Then what? Mission or no mission, the Shards will eat you alive," Ditka said. "You've been deemed disposable more times than I've been called a dog."

The communicator buzzed. Cutter's voice sailed over our heads. "Wise Counsel, we await your signal."

"We gotta get them out of here," Ditka growled.

"Go," I said. "Lark first."

Lark stepped away from the gate. Her golden eyes shone with tears. "Stashya."

"What?" I whispered. "What about Stacia?"

"She wants Stacia to raise her eggs. To teach them to sing," Mike said. "She's staying behind."

"Maybe that's best," Ditka said. "She's injured, her mate dead. Besides, she has to give the signal to seek."

"No!" I yelled at Lark. "That's not best!"

Lark butted me toward the transporter, crying in pain as she flapped her busted wings. I butted her back—gently, so not to hurt her. "We came up here together; we'll go down together."

"Scott," Mike whispered. "Both her wings are broken. It won't work, not this time."

"Probably not," I said. "But hey—I'm in if she is." I wore my game face but fear rippled through me.

One moment I was flying, the next I was falling.

And this time the ground was two miles away.

26

WHiLE MiKE YAMMERED AND pro-tested, I blindsided him through the gate. "You go now!" I yelled to Ditka.

He stood full-length and licked my face. "You're a brave man."

"Cripes, no wet stuff," I said. "Say hi to Barnabus for me. And be nice to my pop." After he had disappeared, I switched off the gate and shoved it under my arm.

I opened the door to the outside. The air sucked out of my lungs but I managed to force a smile at Lark. She whistled back. I heaved the transporter gate off the edge. In a minute, it would hit the ground in Willard Forest and shatter into so many pieces that no one would recognize it.

Was the same about to happen to Lark and me?

Her wings hung uselessly, torn by that monster Cutter. Even though I had taken knocks in football that had set my teeth to spinning, I couldn't imagine her agony. Lark sang quietly, trying to tell herself she didn't hurt and she didn't miss her babies. A small wave of warm hope washed over me but the cold trickles of her misery leaked out.

"The game's not over yet," I said. The bungees were where we had left them. I bent down so Lark could climb onto my back. She gasped as she spread her broken wings to be strapped over my arms. I tried to be gentle but I needed to tie her tight or the ground would blast us like a freight train.

When the Lyra was as secure as I could make her, I said, "Give them the signal."

Lark's powerful shout rang through me as it must be ringing through the Shards—a burning desire to go over the goal line, to fly high, to sing loud.

Seek! And be a hero!

I edged to the end of the landing ramp. The wind knocked us back against the door. The command ship rumbled under my feet—departure was seconds away. Staying on the ship would be safer, I thought. Even with the Shards, it would be less insane than jumping off a cliff from two miles up.

But heroes dare to fly, even when their wings are broken.

"Hey Pillsbury!" I shouted to the earth below. "Get ready for the Hail Mary!"

Then I opened my arms, spread Lark's wings, and jumped.

Born to soar, I had never been this low. The mire provided a cool sanctuary. But the muck, it was in my mouth! I couldn't breathe, I couldn't sing. I was drowning, choking. I had flown to the top of the world, only to die in slime. . . .

"Scottie," Ma yelled. "Wake up!"

"Huh?" I snorfled, spitting out mud. No, not mud. Potatoes and gravy!

"That coach works you too hard," Ma grumbled, wiping my face like I was a little kid. I was too tired to stop her. Every bone in my body moaned with exhaustion. "Falling asleep with your head in Thanksgiving dinner!"

"Huh?" I said again, not resisting when Ma took me by the shoulders and steered me upstairs to my bed. I dimly saw her pulling off my sneakers and pulling a blanket over me.

My head was a maze of feathers and flying and turkey and football. Nothing made much sense. Except the song that rattled in my head . . . sometimes echoing from Stacia's violin, sometimes Lark's voice, sometimes my own yodeling.

Seek and be a hero.

I closed my eyes and let the mire . . . no, my bed . . . provide a sanctuary for my tired bones. Lark brushed the hair from my face . . . no, not Lark, Ma. Pop took my hand . . . not Pop, a Centaur, settling me in the muck so my pain would be relieved. *Football isn't everything,* the Centaur said. No, that was Pop. *There's more to life, Scottie, than just football.*

Yes, there is, I mumbled in my dreams. *More than you can even imagine.*

The Shard and the Jong raged at each other, the flashing hands of the Shard and the venom of the Jong whipping up a storm of foaming poison. Then they saw me.

"Wake up, young Schreiber!" John Cutter snarled.

"Sssssssssurrender, Sssssssschreiber!" the Jong hissed.

"Hey you guys! Go see Pillsbury," I mumbled. "I'm too tired. Besides, he has a bigger brain than me."

"Scott, wake up!"

"Go 'way," I mumbled. "Haven't slept, four nights. Flew 'round the world. Tired. Go get Pillsbury's brain . . ."

"Come on, Thirteen." Pillsbury shook my shoulders, banging my head against the mattress. "Wake up."

"Not getting up," I said, pulling the blanket over my head. "Even if the world's coming to an end, can't get up. Too tired."

Mike rolled me onto the floor. My black-and-blue body howled in pain from the hard wood and my fist was halfway to Pillsbury's face when he blurted, "The eggs! They're hatching!"

Five minutes later, with my hair sticking up and my mouth smelling like stale turkey, I was in the backseat of Stacia's car as her dad chauffeured us to Mike's house. "I'm delighted by your interest in science," he said. "And you, Mike . . . glad you're seeing better."

"Humph," I replied, trying to blink away the morning sun. Friday morning. The day after Thanksgiving.

The Super Bowl was only a few hours away. Did it matter anymore?

Stacia's dad dropped us off. "Day off, good time to practice my golf swing," he said, waving good-bye as he drove away.

Stacia and Mike ran around back; I followed with a fast limp, every joint creaking, every muscle popping. My arms felt like I had lifted a thousand sacks of potatoes, but no—I had just flown off the planet and back. As I approached the tree house, music filled the yard. *Welcome,* Lark sang, and the joy was so clear I didn't need Stacia to translate.

Welcome to this world, where you will find tall trees and good friends.

In the tree house, Lark sat on my old pillow. Her wings were patched and splinted.

"Who did that?" I asked with a yawn.

"Dr. Faulkenham," Stacia said. "My parents offered her a thousand dollars to come out on Thanksgiving and fix my broken 'bird' but she did it for free. No questions asked."

"You okay?" I asked Lark. Last night was a blur—plunging through clouds, Lark howling in pain as we tried to fly, me screaming as an alternative to wetting my pants. A hard landing but a landing just the same—Pillsbury caught us as we ripped through the branches of the old elm tree and crashed to his backyard. Then I remembered Mike unstrapping Lark, Ditka taking me home, Ma trying to feed me supper.

"She's okay," Stacia said. "The wings will take a long time to mend but Ditka says the Ursa have competent healers who will help her."

"Can I . . ." I inched closer, not sure if I was being polite or rude. Lark's tired eyes smiled gold at me and I knew she wanted me to look. The three eggs were cracked, pink showing through the purple outer shell. Inside were wet flutters and little peeps.

"Shouldn't we help them?" I asked.

"No," Mike said. "They've got to do it themselves. It makes them stronger."

We sat, listening to Lark's music, watching the eggs open, one tiny crack at a time. Then, a miracle as a little head appeared. Confused, tiny blinking eyes. Lark kissed her child's face, then smiled at us. "Stashya," she sang. The baby sang it back in a hummingbird whisper. "Stashya."

"She's naming them," Mike said. "The first one is Stashya."

The next head popped through. Twittering and curious, the baby's eyes shone, its head turning, looking for its mother. "Mykkk Dykka," Lark sang. "Mykkk Dykka," the little Lyra answered. Pillsbury reached for Ditka; the big Sirian allowed his ears to be scratched.

Lark cooed and cleaned Stashya and Mykkk Dykka as they hopped on her stomach. The two little ones were curious, happy, healthy—unaware that they had been used like footballs in an inter-galactic tag match.

The last egg rocked as the baby inside struggled to get out. Its tiny shrieks drowned out the happy music from Lark and her two hatchlings.

"He's slow." I reached out, wanting to help him along.

Stacia pulled my hand back. "Give him a chance." She smiled. "He'll figure it out."

BAM! The last egg shattered with a crack. The baby Lyra stepped out, shook his head clear, and hopped onto Lyra. "Cherro," she sang. He pushed through his brother and sister and rubbed against her face. "Cherro," he bellowed.

I smiled, happy for Lark. Then turned my head away. My eyes were wet—I must be allergic to baby birds.

"Scott," Stacia said.

"That's okay," I whispered. "No one said she has to name one after me."

"Listen closer."

Stacia turned me back to Lark, now murmuring to all three babies. Happiness spilled out of the tree house and I knew the whole neighborhood would soon be dancing. "Stashya, Mykkk Dykka, and Cherro," she sang.

Stacia. Mike-Ditka. But Cherro?

"Hero," Stacia whispered. "You, Scott Schreiber—you are Lark's hero. Just like her mate Herald was. Cherro—hero."

My brain exploded with happiness, the whirl of dreams finally coming clear. "Tell her!" I gasped, breathless with excitement. "He's alive! All this time, it wasn't my broken head or bad dreams! It was Herald! He's alive and he's hiding on Centaur—in the Great Swamp, with his friends taking care of him. He's waiting to be rescued, waiting for her,

182

waiting for his children. Tell her, Stacia!"

Stacia laughed. "You just did, Scott. Look."

Lark sang the music of the stars through her golden tears. *Joy to the world.*

27

NICK THORPE'S FAT NOSE AND BLACK eye knocked the hero right out of me.

All of Ashby streamed into the stands, ready to cheer us to a Super Bowl victory that Friday afternoon. Game time was still an hour away but the crowd rocked and the band, with Stacia wailing away on a saxophone, pounded out one spirit song after another.

As I jogged the length of the field, trying to warm my battered muscles and aching bones, I saw Nick hanging over the front bleachers. No sneer or smirk, a simple wave. "Good luck!" he yelled.

The Mighty Schreiber—I was a hero of the skies but still a slime on the ground. I grabbed Coach Tremblay out of his pregame coach's huddle. "Gotta talk to you," I said.

"Later," he growled.

"Now," I growled back. "I don't think I can play this game."

"Move it!" Coach screamed, and I ran my sore bones off the field and into his office.

Mr. Goodrich and my parents met us there.

"What's the matter?" my mother yelled.

"Not now, Marge," Pop growled.

Outside, Keras, LeSieur, and Pillsbury paced the hall. Crisostamo, Tenore, and Hardy took turns peering in through the blinds on Coach's window. Shattuck would have his ear pressed to the door, listening to every sorry word.

"You have something to tell me, Mr. Schreiber?" Goodrich asked.

"Yep," I said. "I . . . uh . . ." The words wouldn't come. The walls shook with cheers from the field, almost deafening even here, inside the school.

"Spit it out!" Coach yelled. "We don't have all day! We got a game to win!" His voice was harsh but his watery blue eyes darted from me to Goodrich and back.

I told it all so fast, I couldn't stop it once I started. "Mr. Goodrich, Nick lied to take the blame for me. I punched him first because he was bugging me. I deserved to be suspended, not him, and I know I probably can't play football because I punched him and I lied about it afterwards. But he was making fun

185

of my nest and he didn't have the right. I am very sorry. He was a jerk but I was a bigger jerk."

I glanced at my parents. Ma's eyes filled with tears. Pop's face was stone. "I'm sorry," I said.

Even with the noise from the field, the silence in Coach's office fell like a sheet of ice. Hard and cold.

Then Mr. Goodrich laughed. "You think I was born yesterday, Scott? I knew you punched Nick first."

"You did? Then you shouldn't cover for me," I mumbled. "It's not right."

"I didn't cover for you," he said. "You've never been in trouble before. So, according to our guidelines, a detention is the proper offense for a first skirmish. That's what I gave you."

"But Nick got suspended. I thought that was the punishment for smacking someone."

"He did get suspended. And because he was trying to spare you, I suspended him only for one day. Nick has a record spotted with black marks, mostly from causing fights with his smart mouth. He had already been warned the next episode would be very serious, worth a three-day suspension. But he finally realized that the trouble he stirs up has wider ramifications than just some shouting and shoving for his own amusement. He learned that by provoking you into something you don't normally do he could be hurting the whole school."

186

"So, you didn't let me off because I'm a football player?"

"I didn't let you off at all. I gave you the proper discipline for someone with a clean record. And I let Nick's lie stand because he was trying to do something right for once. In a wrong way—but I suspected you would figure it out soon enough."

"You did?" I said.

"Sure." Mr. Goodrich laughed. "All that football talent and muscle don't fool me, Scott. There's a good kid under those pads and helmet. It makes you stronger to figure some things out for yourself. I took a chance that you would, and you did."

The guilt washed out of me in a rush. Suddenly, despite my bumps and bruises, I felt incredibly strong and incredibly ready to play a game.

"So I can play? Honestly play?"

"Go get 'em, Thirteen," Goodrich said.

Ma tried to smother me in hugs but Pop got there before her. "I'm sorry, Pop," I whispered as he shook my hand.

"You're a good man, son," he whispered back. Then he hugged me.

"What're we gonna do today?" Coach said as he and I stepped into the hallway.

"WIN!" I shouted.

"WIN!" my team roared back.

"Not so fast." Mr. FitzPatrick pushed through my teammates.

"Problem with winning, Mr. FitzSpu— FitzPatrick?" Coach asked.

"Problem with cheating, *Mis*ter Tremblay. I've just been informed that this man Cutter was a fraud!" he yelled. "The Caraviellos have sworn out a warrant for his arrest. Apparently he stole a very expensive violin. Don't know what he wanted with that dirty nest of Mr. Schreiber's but we can no longer assume it to be a rare find sanctioned by the EPA. Therefore, Mr. Schreiber's grade must revert to an F. And that means disqualification from athletic activities."

Hardy pedaled over Clark, wanting to take FitzPatrick down. Coach clenched his fists, resisting the same impulse. "Twenty minutes before our first Super Bowl?" he hissed, grinding his teeth so hard I thought sparks would fly.

I slumped against the wall, too tired to fight. I *had* screwed up the science project, and although the nest was the most amazing thing that had ever passed through the halls of this school, I couldn't prove it.

"Mr. FitzPatrick!" Mike Pillsbury yelled.

"Yes, Mr. Pillsbury?"

"I'm sure you weren't aware that Scott spent all

of Thanksgiving tracking down the maker of the nest."

"Scottie?" my mother squealed.

"Not now, Marge," my father said in a low voice. Ma went dead silent for the second time in ten minutes.

"No, I wasn't aware of that," said FitzPatrick. "Nor can I believe such an absurd story unless I have some proof."

Mike grinned and reached into his playbook. "How's this for proof?" He handed FitzPatrick a printout of the digital photo he had taken two hours ago at the tree house. Fortunately, Lark's human-like face and arms weren't visible. Bending over Stashya, Mykk-Dykka, and Cherro, she was a mass of feathers. And I sat next to her, a goofy smile on my face.

"What an amazing bird!" FitzPatrick said. "Truly amazing. And so big. Any idea what species she is? Is she still around? Can I see her?"

"Uh . . ." I stumbled. What to say without revealing her alien origins? I wouldn't wish neutralization on anyone, even the Potato.

Pillsbury came to the rescue. "Scott checked it out in a bird book. Identified her as a member of the lark family. But she's gone, flew off with her babies."

FitzPatrick turned to me, his eyes glittering.

"Wonderful work, Mr. Schreiber. A-plus work. Consider yourself passed."

I wiped the grin off my face in an instant. As I tell Pillsbury, grinning over an A-plus is an invitation to a whupping. Besides, we had a game to play.

"Come on, men!" I yelled. "Ain't nothing between us and that Super Bowl trophy except the goal line."

28

WE WEREN'T THE ONLY TEAM THAT HAD
come ready to play. The Pepperell Boars steamrolled
us in the first half, pounding through our front line
like we were ghosts who couldn't *boo* a kitten. At the
half, we were behind 14–0. In the locker room,
Coach ranted and raved; I pleaded and begged;
Pillsbury reasoned and calculated. But we couldn't
seem to raise the team to a fighting spirit.

Pepperell was just too good and I was just so
darned tired.

There's more to life than football, Pop had said.
But this moment belonged to football and this
moment was one of the many moments I was born
for. I chased the team back to the field after the half,
grunting and growling, trying to get them fired up.

The Ashby side was silent. The band had

stopped, the cheerleaders had quieted, and the crowd was still. *All ready for our funeral,* I thought. Then I heard it. Clear as a bell, strong as steel, happy as a lark—Stacia stood on our bench, fiddling away on her patched-up violin. The notes were scratchy and squeaky but the message couldn't be clearer.

Win, Ashby, Win!

She fiddled through the whole second half—through the band playing, the announcer broadcasting, the players yelling, the crowd chanting.

In the third quarter, DuCharme kicked a field goal from an impossible distance and we closed the gap, 14–3. Early in the fourth quarter, after Tenore and Clark had sacked the Pepperell QB for the fourth time, the poor guy stumbled off the field claiming to hear bells.

This fired up the Pepperell defense, who drove us back into our territory. We battled back and forth and time clicked down until there was less than a minute left.

"What does Coach say?" I asked Pillsbury.

"Pray," he said.

"Okay." I laughed. "Pray it is."

I sent Pillsbury downfield. *Way* downfield. Through the maze of blue-and-scarlet-shirted players, his skinny butt danced and twittered. I whipped the football with every ounce of my strength. After a day of flying, my muscles squealed and moaned but that football flew high and true. Ma screamed out her lungs: "A Hail Mary pass!" Pepperell's safety rushed to cover the kid with the skinny legs and sports goggles. I heard Pillsbury's "Oomph" from ninety yards away as the football buried in his gut, then there was nothing but a wall of sound and Keras pounding my helmet. "Touchdown!" he shouted. "The geek did it."

Clark kicked the point after and I did the math: 14–10 with ten seconds left. I called time and ran to the sidelines.

"Listen up, Thirteen," Coach growled, but I brushed past him. I leaped onto the bench and waved my arms at the crowd. Palms down, down. The cheerleaders picked it up—QUIET—and our side of the field went silent.

I pointed at Stacia. "Play!" I said. "No one but her!" She turned redder than my shirt and blinked faster than my heart was racing but she smiled and continued to scratch her Lyra-stringed fiddle.

The whistle blew and we ran out to the field, no play in hand. Pepperell had possession and were likely to just sit on the football. "Get that ball," I roared, and Crisostamo plowed through five Pepperell thugs, steaming for the quarterback.

Fumble! I saw Shattuck and Monroe whiz over the blockers, then lost them in a tumble of Ashby red and Pepperell blue. When the whistle blew and the pile cleared, LeSieur came up spitting grass and clutching the football.

Three yards from the end zone. Two seconds left in the game. Four points behind—a three-point field goal would do us no good.

I gathered the men in the huddle. Pillsbury ran in with Coach's play. "Quarterback sneak," he said.

"No," I said. My body ached and moaned. I couldn't bear every attacker coming down my throat. I had to hand the ball off, just to spare myself. "I can't do it. I'm outta gas."

"You have to, Scott. No one else can pull it off."

I pulled Mike's helmet to mine. "I'll fall apart," I said. "After the past few days . . ." Suddenly, a light flashed above us. The sun was afternoon bright, the sky was clear blue, but somehow I was seeing stars. Not stars, one star, shooting up to the heavens.

"Lark?"

"The Ursa, taking her and the babies to Centaura to get Herald."

"It wasn't a dream, was it, Mike?"

He slapped my helmet. "Nope, Thirteen, it wasn't a dream. And neither is that Super Bowl trophy."

Some sneak. Pepperell knew it was coming. No other play made sense here. My blockers positioned in front of me. Over their backs, the Pepperell defense looked like a herd of blue bulls, ready to stampede me into ground beef.

I tapped my foot, shouted the signals, and suddenly knew—as certain as the music of the stars—that I had one jump left in me. If I wanted to, I could leap that front line as if they were a row of daisies—just jump into that end zone and claim our victory.

But as the ball snapped into my gut, I kept my feet on the ground. Pepperell players surged from every side but I would not fly over them. No, I was going to push my way through, batter those bodies back and claim that touchdown with my own two feet.

After all—I was the Mighty Schreiber.